Wiz

Duos

Book 1

Wiz Duos

Book 1

David Gullen & Ben Wright

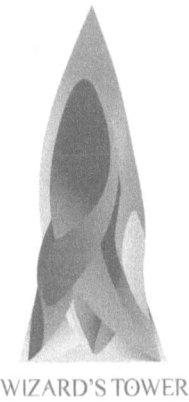

WIZARD'S TOWER

Wizard's Tower Press

Rhydaman, Cymru

Wiz Duos

Book 1

Stories by David Gullen & Ben Wright

Edited by Roz Clarke & Joanne Hall

Cover art by Roz Clarke
Cover design by Ben Baldwin

Book design by Cheryl Morgan

First published by Wizard's Tower Press,
May 2025

ISBN: 978-1-913892-96-8

http://wizardstowerpress.com/

Contents

FOREWORD

By
Roz Clarke & Joanne Hall

Often when we're reading submissions we know we're looking for something, but we're not quite sure what that something is until we see it. We found that with 'To Sail The Interstice', which is a novella so crammed with big ideas that we marvelled at Ben Wright's ability to fit them all into a work of this length, when there are at least three potential novels in here.

We follow the unlikely trio of main characters from world to world, from the coasts and jungles where giant robotic factories contaminate the land, to an immense cathedral held together with song and the mysterious underworld that may bring it crashing down, to a band of misfits and broken travellers, stranded in the desert after an air crash, who must pull together to survive.

Ben weaves these three connected threads together with the skill of a master craftsperson. It probably, technically, shouldn't work but it does and the novella is all the more joyful because of Ben's ambition.

It's here we find a connection with David Gullen's 'The God Road', with its similar theme of characters cast out of their impossible city into a treacherous wasteland. Jo especially has an editorial weakness for Great Big Dead Things and David's GBDT is literally the size of a city. He says that he was inspired by the idea of whalefall; of the communities and ecosystems that arise on the bodies of dead leviathans when they fall to the bottom of the sea. Except that in this case the leviathan has fallen onto dry land, and it's not a whale, but what the inhabitants of this body-city believe to be a god.

The characters in this story are a compelling mixture of alien and familiar: nothing like us, but relatable in all the essential ways. David brings us a story full of strange terrors, not least of which are the dangers that ones friends and allies can present when a group of people are under strain. Through the lens of the weird and mysterious, he reflects on humanity and the pursuit of security and love.

The God Road

David Gullen

DAVID GULLEN

THE GOD ROAD

1. City of Flesh

A restlessness builds in a city when the end is near. Scouts are sent out, then war bands. Quiet schisms become vocal, strident. The scholarly debates of a generation past are now knife-fights in the taverns and alleyways.

On one such uncertain day Myxini priests celebrate the dedication of their last temple to the universal solitary, the creator above. LucusAna, adopted scion of the opposing Aganathans, reluctantly makes his way along Great Heart Road, the city's main thoroughfare. He heads towards the sounds and aromas of festival. He doesn't want to go, he knows he doesn't belong, to his mind Myxini doctrine is close to abomination. But by convention all are welcome and, more importantly, he is very hungry. Despite this profound moral compromise he tells himself he still has standards. He will eat Myxini temple flesh because he refuses to gnaw the walls.

Thank the good gods, when he arrives he sees CharAncho is there too. His closest friend, they have shared in each other's moult-feasts and are sworn as one. She watches the Myxini guards with that quiet smile of hers. Her second arms are clasped low on her belly plates, one of her first hands rests on the hilt of the long knife scabbarded on her chest harness. It is a long, narrow, and sharp-tipped blade of blackish purple godbone, made for mischief, made for slipping between the overlap of throat scales or side plates. It has seen some use.

All weapons are banned from temples, a convention now widely ignored. Myxini guards return CharAncho's steady gaze as she walks towards them. Their tails are low, they stand relaxed and at ease with their impossibly expensive godsteel knives and gaffs in their own first hands.

Her look asks them who will deny a bold Aganathan warrior their eating-knife at a temple feast?

Nobody, apparently.

"Ana." CharAncho looks almost as relieved to see LucusAna as he is to see her. It's always good to have someone watching your back, especially these days. Especially in a Myxini temple on dedication day, even if the food is free.

"CharAncho."

"All is One."

"The One is All."

They make the sign, fingers of their second hands interlaced, the Aganathan weave. Side by side they walk past the temple guards into an open crowd of Myxini celebrants and believers, and those like them who are simply here to eat.

Away through the bustle LucusAna sees his long-time neighbour, the old toy-maker, DanDocin. He lives alone, though in cycles past his children filled his apartment with happy energy. He stands uncertainly while the crowd mills by. LucusAna thinks the old fellow looks like he himself feels.

"A pleasure to see you, DanDocin. I hope you are well, that your family is well."

DanDocin regards him with blank incomprehension.

LucusAna feels slightly foolish. "We are neighbours. I'm LucusAna."

"LucusAna, LucusAna," DanDocin softly punches his right fist into his left palm. "Ah, one flight up and two across."

It is two flights up and one across, but LucusAna does not correct him. "You have come to eat?" Godflesh is city, home, and food, whatever else the foolish Myxini believe.

DanDocin starts, as if he has just remembered something. "I just wanted to see what they've done."

A hundred cycles past DanDocin worked as a flesh mason and carved the finials, interior gables and buttresses supporting the roof of Ro's third shrine, that vast and multi-storied hall. Vast yet tiny compared to the titanic mass of fallen godflesh they hollowed it from, city to twenty generations who excavated and ate as they multiplied. When age meant DanDocin could no longer grip his skives, gouges, and groovers he retired to his workshop and entertained himself making toys for first-moult children.

Though his words come slowly DanDocin is articulate. "I like the modern deep-pattern style. In my day I never thought we took enough time. I felt to honour our beliefs we should create our finest work, but back then it was grab, grab space in the city while we could." He peers up, "For all this is misguided Myxini inspiration, the craftsmanship is fine."

Above them, supported on graceful columns of marbled godflesh, arches a vaulted roof, an intricate filigree of carved meat and bone backlit by swirls of tethered livelights. Complex plays of soft blue light and dense shadow drift across the godflesh floor and race up the walls. It is quite beautiful. LucusAna does his best to admire the workmanship and ask questions, but DanDocin has lapsed back into silence.

LucusAna is starving. "Come, let's eat."

DanDocin shrinks back towards the wall and the shadows. "I'll stay here." He flaps his hands at the crowds. "All these people, I'm not used to it."

"I'll fetch you something."

DanDocin thanks him with a gratitude bordering on pathetic. LucusAna feels both sad and irritated. Aganathan belief is strength; the old fellow is weak.

CharAncho waits impatiently. Her gaze takes in the splits and cracks on DanDocin's age-darkened lateral plates, and the archaic phrases carved there. "Who is that shabby old fellow?"

"A neighbour. The local toy-maker. He used to be a flesh mason at our temples."

CharAncho laughs. "Can he even remember his own name?"

LucusAna says nothing. He doesn't like it, but CharAncho is right. DanDocin is turning into a husk, the time approaches when he will be turned away from even Aganathan tables.

The tailings of this final Myxini temple, excavated, hollowed and carved from the last great mass of uncut godflesh in the city, will feed the population for two hundred cycles. LucusAna suspects that well before that it will be exclusively Myxini faction who dine on their temple's spoil. At that point there will be civil war.

A procession of Myxini faithful winds through the crowd, swinging bone thuribles of god-blood incense. Led by a troupe of drone-flute players their segmented bodies sway in a sinuous rhythmic stamp. CharAncho waits for them to pass then sets off towards the bounty tables. As always a path opens in front of her. LucusAna follows, half-amused, convinced that CharAncho isn't even aware of what's happening. Paths have always opened for her. She doesn't threaten, she doesn't glare, people just get out of her way. One day it's probably going to get her killed.

The tables support an array of large oval platters piled with cuts of faintly iridescent godflesh, the meat sliced so thin you can almost see through it. A garnish of squat lobster and soft coral borders each dish, each one of which has been sawn cross-cut through mighty fingerbones, then polished and chased around the lip with some Myxini creed.

LucusAna reads the inscription on the nearest platters with unease: "The Willing Sacrifice"; "An Offering of Flesh."

In these two phrases and seven words is the essence of the difference between Myxini and Aganathan. Exactly what is this titanic entity which generations of them had turned into a city, hollowed out, mined and carved and eaten? Was it an actual fragment of the Great Solitary above, willingly calved from their own immortal body and given form to descend and sustain its worshippers? Or was it, as the Aganathans believe, the fallen corpse of some outcast, struck down in heaven's eternal war?

CharAncho shoulders past, takes one of the larger cuts and consumes it with quick snips and chops of her mandibles. She moans with pleasure, lost in the moment. LucusAna pushes aside his existential concerns and follows her lead.

Unsullied godflesh is soft and sweet, each mouthful a melting delight. LucusAna groans and closes his eyes. CharAncho laughs and reaches for another slice. LucusAna looks around, then quickly scoops cuts of godflesh into his harness satchel with both first hands.

"All are welcome, all are welcome." Myxini sacerdotes move among the crowd, apparently benign, watching, counting, noting names. "Even you, LucusAna. Denier, heretic, apostate."

It is GalaTheo, his crimson god-skin sash showing him to be newly elevated into the clerics of the Myxini third order.

There was a time when LucusAna and GalaTheo leaned on the bar of one or other holy tavern, brow to brow, snorting and giggling at each other's drunken insults:

"God-Scoffer."

"Heretic."

"Credulous Myxini."

"Aganathan denier."

LucusAna the foundling, a rejected child of unknown provenance adopted by poor Aganathans; GalaTheo, born to the Myxini high path, his belief no more than a means to an end. Somehow they were friends.

Shoulder to bumping shoulder they ambled through the arterial side-streets, down Great Heart Road, tripping over valved intersections to the three-way divide that took them their separate ways.

"One day you'll come to us," GalaTheo said at times like these. "I know it."

"Maybe I will," LucusAna would say, not wanting to hurt his friend's feelings.

"Spiritual brothers," GalaTheo said on one such occasion with drunken seriousness, then fell over his own feet onto his back.

LucusAna rolled him over and hauled him up, and they clung to each other.

"See? Spirishual brothers," GalaTheo slurred. And in that moment they were, and ever would be. Myxini and Aganathan creeds were just differences of opinion and nothing more.

Now, despite his smiles, there is such a cold certainty to GalaTheo's words they hurt worse than a knife under a belly plate. Beneath the pain LucusAna feels a deep sorrow for what once was and can never be again. And his heart grows hard, for the Myxini are wrong, their thoughts are wrong, and he knows they will not change. After an unpleasant moment of stillness and silence GalaTheo moves on. LucusAna resumes eating.

#

Celebrations have barely begun to wind down when Osedax, the gigantic parent of the Bone Clan nomads, arrives outside the city walls with their white worm army.

Faced with such a threat Myxini and Aganathans put aside their differences to present a united front.

From the crowded ramparts of the doorless walls LucusAna looks down on the Bone Clan horde, a vast writhe of pale monstrosities. Some are legless and some, to LucusAna's mind, have far too many limbs. Osedax, both queen and king, has made camp on a low rise, surrounded by their sub-queens, courtiers and drones. All stand inside a great circle of black pennants that stream in the wind blowing steadily at their backs. Beyond them a grey plain rolls away into deepening gloom in a series of low undulations.

Osedax, whose army has been feeding on itself, glides forwards. Their attendant child-worms, segmented and blind, whose jawless mouths can gnaw through mudstone and godbone itself, cascade from their sides and ripple forwards in a pale wave.

Up on the wall, Albicaud, the Myxini Pontiff, and MakuraMazara, vice-philosopher of the Aganathans, prepare to descend in two of the crane-baskets that hang over the high Godflesh walls. Buttressed on the inside by unworked ribs, braced and cross-braced by spars of grey godbone, the walls are no longer what they once were. Despite armed patrols, cycle by cycle they have been pared down, made thinner and thinner by the growing population.

MakuraMazara beckons to LucusAna's group and they, with trepidation, answer her summons.

"Attend me," MakuraMazara says. "Be my guard, my honour, my life."

CharAncho is ready for this, LucusAna less so. Both take the pennanted godbone spears handed them. He aches to touch it and test its edge, but doesn't dare. A dozen others crowd onto the platform, armed and ready. The gate is closed, the platform shudders and begins to descend.

LucusAna has never been outside the city. Few have, there is no reason. Nothing lives on the endless grey silt except the scavengers of the lost, the weak, and the deluded. Scavengers who do not care if their prey is alive or dead.

The city is all, and provides all, but godflesh grows scarce and the population just grows. Myxini and Aganathans end-lessly manoeuvre for advantage. The Myxini know their true strength is in their belief that God provides from their own flesh and will not abandon them. Hope, as everyone knows, dies last. Cycle by cycle more people fill the Myxini temples while Aganathan numbers dwindle.

"This is still our city. You are not welcome here." Albicaud tells Osedax.

MakuraMazara says, "Withdraw, or face the conse-quences. You come too early."

"Yet the wind calls and here I am," Osedax says. Three hundred transparent eggs, each as big as LucusAna's tho-rax, are embedded in five brood-channels along their back. Inside them transparent larvae spin and wriggle, dragging their dark yolk sacks with them. "The wind says 'Come, for this city is ripe.'" Osedax's gesture encompasses drones, sub-queens, courtiers, and army. "As the wind speaks, so we obey."

LucusAna grimaces and flinches under the sheer pressure of having no roof over his head for the first time in his life. Under his feet the mudstone stretches away forever. Above him the sky from which gods descend, and across which swarms of wild livelights pulse, is an infinite blank darkness. He glances at CharAncho who stands motionless, rigid with effort. The other guards jerk and flinch with their own ticks as they fight for self-control.

"Sorry, sorry." One of them crouches lower and lower then abruptly scuttles back to the shelter of the crane basket, walled and roofed. Their failure renews LucusAna's determination. Faith is strength.

Osedax gives a signal. Ever-eager drones scuttle left and right. Each carries a black flag on a long pole. Behind them the bone-worm army divides into three companies, the head and pincers formation designed to encircle and destroy.

Excited by the massed movement, wild livelights surge upwards, bells pulsing, bathing everyone in sharp-edged light.

LucusAna grips his spear with his first hands. The odds here are hundreds to one. Today is not the day he thought he would die, it is very unexpected and he is utterly unprepared. Yet, like Osedax, the moment has arrived. *All is One,* he mouths to himself, *The One is All.* Beside him, CharAncho seems unperturbed. She lifts her armoured head and quietly laughs.

As if it were a signal the city ramparts fill with half a thousand warriors bearing nets and tridents and hooked knives. They number less than a quarter of Osedax's army, but if the bone-worms attack head-on, they will be enough.

Osedax subsides and folds multiple spindle-arms across the segments of their pale belly. "We can wait," they say. "We shall wait."

A great gust of relief blows through LucusAna, stronger than the wind that endlessly courses the grey lands. Today they will not fight, today he will live.

\#

Back behind the city walls MakuraMazara thanks and dismisses most of her guard, but not LucusAna and Cha-rAncho.

"Walk with me," she says, and leads them to her private rooms in the primal Aganathan temple to Ro, Egg of the Cosmos.

On the way MakuraMazara chatters about this and that: gossip about Aganathan power-politics; duplicitous Myxini scheming; that her brother is now a father too.

"It's not the ideal time to become a parent, but hey-ho."

Somewhat awed to be spoken to in such a familiar way, LucusAna finds himself relaxing in her company. She seems kind and attentive, she listens to his questions and answers them, she has a good grasp of detail. This is all he has ever wanted, to be accepted, to have a home. To belong.

He also sees the hunger on the streets. Everywhere, on the walls and even along the less heavily trampled edges of the streets, are gouge marks where godflesh has been skived away to be eaten. The walls of some lesser bye-ways are now membrane-thin, the edges of the paths worked down into deep gutters filled with a nameless and reeking deep green seep. Children of the second moult crouch there and watch with calculating eyes as they pass by.

There are no such problems in the Aganathan temples, as guards patrol inside and out. The fluting on the squat pillars, scroll-work on the pedestal and base, and the bas-relief friezes narrating the deeds of Ro are all as clean and clear as the day they were first cut from the purple and white marbled godflesh.

There is plenty of food in MakuraMazara's rooms. Their hands interlock in the weave before they sit and eat in silence, each meal a private communion with the fallen gift, the offering, the death. All is one.

"There are rumours," MakuraMazara says when they have finished. "Rumours of a new godfall, far along the road."

Godfall, that rarest and luckiest of gifts. LucusAna and CharAncho share a sudden glance. A road? There is a road? From where to where?

"Our scouts rove far beyond the city walls, explorers and way-finders," MakuraMazara tells them. "I meet with them from time to time." She mentions a name, the scout called AmkaTan, a living legend.

She reaches down and lifts a pair of long-handled, single-edged blades onto the table. The black godbone handles are inscribed with Aganathan creed, the blades, as long as LucusAna's forearm, are of dappled silver-on-grey metal. Godsteel. They are items of astonishing value, the steel reforged from one of only three god-blades ever found in the history of the people of the cities. The Aganathan blade was found lodged deep in the body of the descended which became the city three times removed from the current one. Myxini temples have held the other two far longer.

"You passed a test standing beyond the city walls, you endured the open sky. I want you to go and find that new city. Claim it for me, for all Aganathans. For Ro."

LucusAna wants that blade so very much, but he hesitates.

To go outside the city again.

He asks himself if he is scared and the answer is yes, more than a little. But CharAncho has already taken one of the weapons. She holds it with admiration then makes a few short sweeps and thrusts.

"Of course," she says, and LucusAna knows he will follow. They have shared, they are as one.

#

Before they have finished their preparations one of the older Myxini temples collapses, a near-liquid infolding of pillars and roof that pulls down the muti-tiered homes of the holy poor who live above. Many die, more are hurt, and Aganathan sabotage is loudly proclaimed. Denial counts for nothing. That internal pillars and walls have been robbed of strength, skived and skived again by the starving poor, counts for nothing. The collapse is the excuse, the implicit declaration of the civil war everyone knows is coming.

The first LucusAna knows about any of this is when an armed mob rampages through the Aganathan quarter he lives in. Horrified, he stares down through the window space at a roaring, violent press streaming below. Myxini pennants hang from godbone tridents. Head-catchers, spearheads and knives are already bloodied.

He sees his Aganathan neighbours dragged out and dismembered, men and women roaring with rage and fear. Children of first moult are flung into the air and speared on godbone poles. Screaming with delight, the mob stamp and smash Aganathan eggs. Dark yolk mixed with blood drips from their arms and faces.

Old DanDocin is hauled from his workshop, his simple toys gleefully trampled. There is a moment when he is hoisted, splayed above the mob, and his eyes meet LucusAna's. He looks more confused than frightened, he shows no pain as knives are driven into his body, separating his joints. His look says he neither understands what is happening to him, or why. A terrible communion connects him to LucusAna, then he is gone, subsumed into the howling mob. What lived and breathed moments ago is now just flopping meat.

Faces turn upwards. Arms point, weapons too. LucusAna is seen. In blind panic he grabs the godsteel blade and runs for his life. Up, he goes, into the cramped over-tunnels below the city roof, where first ingress into the city of flesh was cut generations past.

Frantic and terrified, he descends some distance away and connects with a group of Aganathan guards. Every one of them is wounded, chest plates cracked, plate seams punctured, their faces and first arms smeared with blood not their own. Discipline still holds, they are a unit.

"RingenZaem!" He is desperately glad to see someone he knows, a veteran guard with a reputation approaching CharAncho's. The academic, AnphraJon, is there too, looming over everyone like an adult over third moult youngsters. An old friend from the tertium where they studied creed, history, and theories of mutable truth, he is unarmed and probably incapable of wielding arms. All he carries is a large satchel filled with notes and papers slung on a belt between his first and second arms. He is the gentlest person LucusAna has ever known.

"This way. Quickly." RingenZaem leads them forwards, alert and cautious. LucusAna falls in beside her.

"What in all that's holy is going on?"

AnphraJon presses in close behind. "They're killing everyone."

"Everyone Aganathan." RingenZaem rattles her side plates. "Not us, not today."

"Ay-ha!" Her squad clatter weapons against carapaces in agreement. It is a reassuringly aggressive sound.

"Can you use that beautiful thing?" RingenZaem says, eyeing LucusAna's godsteel blade.

"If I have to, yes."

"Good. Because that's going to happen."

"Only if I have to."

RingenZaem leads the way towards the first temple, the heart of all things Aganathan. They are almost there when a flag waving Myxini mob boils out of a side passage and blocks their path. RingenZaem's squad formates quickly and smoothly, a wall of armour and weapons, tails raised. Terminal plates hiss warning.

The front rows of the mob don't hesitate. They hurl themselves forwards in an undisciplined howling rush.

Rooted to the spot, all LucusAna can do is watch them die.

AnphraJon grabs him with all four hands and drags him round. Behind them, two Myxini temple guards and four masked third order priests are about to fall on their rear.

"You're going to have to!"

The guards rush in, tails high. LucusAna draws his blade, godsteel sings free of the scabbard.

The guards falter at the sight of it but the priests push past, screaming blasphemy. For all his practice, LucusAna has never fought a real fight. He can duel all right, but that is one on one, a game. Yet the priests know nothing. They crowd each other, they obstruct the guards, who really can fight, they hack and hew with their bone blades without thought for their own safety.

The godsteel is magnificent. LucusAna lops a hand here, a leg there. Behind him, AnphraJon clutches his satchel to his body like a shield and shrieks at each blow. "Watch your left, Ana! Now the right!"

LucusAna sees the danger. He slashes down, a controlled, close blow. The godsteel slices into the priest's mask, through brain and eye, opening face and mouth.

"Ay-ay-ay!" AnphraJon yelps as the priest's cheek and mandibles slop to the ground. They spit blood, gargle something incomprehensible, then collapse into a heap of kicking limbs.

A kind of controlled terror grips LucusAna. He has killed; he is a killer. Is his life worth more than that priest? To himself, yes, vastly. "Stop," he roars. "I *will* do that again."

Two masked priests press forwards, one hangs back. A guard barrels through, head low, weapons high, and it is as if LucusAna watches himself from above as he takes a dancing step to one side, rolls his grip, and slices up hard between thorax and abdomen, cutting through side plates, through muscle and nerves.

The guard is down and screaming, LucusAna is drenched in blood. He can smell it, taste it, it is in his mouth. He howls, appalled at what he is doing. At what he must do.

The dying guard clutches at him with mortal strength. A kick makes him stumble. Then the two priests pile onto him, blades in their first hands, second hands fumbling across his face, his eyes, and clutching for his weapon. He feels their bone knives sliding across his back plates, seeking the soft gaps between.

Somewhere AnphraJon is begging them to stop. LucusAna knows the young academic is incapable of helping and accepts the fact. The fight has become a physical tussle, two against one. The priest's masked faces are close against his, their breath wuffs onto his face. He feels a knife point push home with terrific disabling pain. He cannot move.

I will not die. Not today. Not like this. LucusAna twists away from the knife, heaves and flexes. One of his secondary arms breaks with a bright, flaring pain that fills his eyes with white light. He turns his head, drives it into a priest's face and bites through their mask so hard his mandibles meet. Briefly, the weight on him eases. His sword arm comes free and he stabs and slashes blindly. Then he is up and chopping without finesse or style, hacking again and again.

The two priests are more than dead, they are butchered. LucusAna stands in their dripping ruin and screams at the remaining priest and guard.

"Protect me." The priest backs away and the guard comes to their side. LucusAna feigns a rush and the priest jumps back, then turns and flees. As they do, their mask slips aside and LucusAna sees it is his old friend, GalaTheo. Among all the horrors of the day, of everything he has been forced to do simply to continue to live, this is the one thing LucusAna most wishes he could unsee.

Behind him is carnage. RingenZaem's squad has stood and held and the mob has died in piles at their feet. Livelights, spilled from their broken cages, have uncurled their proboscis and are already feeding, sipping, drinking. Laying eggs.

RingenZaem checks LucusAna over. His wounds are bloody but superficial, his arm will mend. "You can walk." It is not a question.

"Yes." LucusAna looks everywhere except at the corpses he has made. He would leave this awful place even if it killed him.

"Then we go." RingenZaem gazes steadily at LucusAna's handiwork. She grips his shoulder. "That was well done."

RingenZaem leads them down a wide vein tunnel, waits, listening, at the junction with a narrower one, then hurries them along it single-file. Part way down, a door cracks open. They slip inside, past a squad of militant Aganathan guards bristling with weapons and aggression. AnphraJon scurries in wild-eyed. RingenZaem, having brought her squad to safety, enters last. The door is closed, barred, and barred again.

LucusAna finds himself in a passageway flanked by side-chapels and meditation cells and realises he is inside Ro's temple, the soulhearth of Aganathan life. He is safe. With that realisation comes quivering aftershock at what he has endured. The press of so many people around him is too much, the babble of voices, the swirling livelights. His broken arm aches abominably. He turns his face to the wall, curls up on the ground and sinks into a fugue. Welcome darkness wraps his mind.

After an unmeasurable period, a moment, a cycle, ten thousand lifetimes, he emerges and looks around with a vision that seems far more acute than normal. He sees the intricate web of capillaries in the godflesh wall; he hears a dozen conversations around him with supernal clarity. By turns he is fascinated with the beating rows of cilia along a hovering livelights's body and the angle and lap of the tool-marks where Aganathan credo has been carved into the side ridges of his own body segments. "From the One, Many." "To Fall is to Rise." "The One is the All." There is profundity there, he is certain, but in that moment it eludes him. He is here, what is done is done, he finds he can live with himself.

The temple has become a fort, a refuge, a city within a city. Despite the great influx of refugees from the pogrom there is some semblance of order, the Aganathan leadership has known this time was coming and have prepared. Under the steady blue-white light of caged livelights, family groups and solitary children fill the chapels and line the walls, silent with trauma and shock. Heavy slabs of godmeat are piled on sleds between the carved pillars and stacked in heaps around the central pit where, in better times, the great bone sphere representing the cosmic egg, smooth, slick, and pale, is pushed by the faithful on its endless circuit.

He thinks of DanDocin, the old toymaker. The look in his eyes in the moment before the mob tore him apart. *See me. I have lived. Now I am gone.* LucusAna vows to never to forget DanDocin, that as long as he himself endures, so does the old toymaker. Having decided, he feels stronger for it.

The central aisles are cleared for action. Squads and bat-talions of Aganathan guards and volunteers militant stand in well-spaced groups. The main door has been sealed, glued and barricaded with godbone scaffold set deep in the flesh of the walls and floor. Off to one side three children grind godmeat in hand-turned mills to feed the livelights.

He finds RingenZaem deep in conversation with a battle-group commander, their thorax bright with the blue paint of command.

"Here he is," RingenZaem says. "The very one."

"You did more than well." The commander studies him with close attention. "You are wounded."

"Leave it to me." RingenZaem leads LucusAna to an empty space in the ranks. There, a surgeon fusses over LucusAna with the haste of the impossibly busy.

"This will hurt, hold still," she says as she cleans then probes the knife wound.

She is right. LucusAna hisses with pain, flexes and clenches his tail, but does not otherwise move.

"It did not penetrate, muscle damage only. Lucky." The surgeon closes the puncture with three stitches. "Arm."

LucusAna cautiously presents his broken arm. The surgeon takes it in her first hands, supporting it with one hand and manipulating the joint behind the break with the other. "The joint's intact." For the first time she makes eye contact. "Lucky again."

LucusAna laughs. Whatever has happened today, he does not feel fortunate. Then, before he can object, the surgeon slices a thin strip from the chitin flange edging one of his tail segments, using a godsteel scalpel in a secondary hand. It is painless, but he cannot help feel affront.

Working quickly the surgeon softens the strip in a steam pot, then moulds and glues it over the break in his arm.

"One more should do it." The surgeon catches LucusAna's look. "You're not final moult?"

"I... No."

"Shame." The surgeon takes another slice from the other side of the same segment. "These cuts and splints would give you a story to tell."

"I suppose so. Thank you."

But the surgeon has moved on, their attention now on the next patient. LucusAna tries his arm and finds it is sound and strong. He looks around and sees RingenZaem heading towards the far end of the temple where a cluster of blue pennants hang. Painted in blue and gold MakuraMazara, the Aganathan vice-philosopher, is there, surrounded by her senior priests and generals.

On his way over LucusAna stumbles across AnphraJon, curled into a ball with his legs and arms folded under his body. All four hands clutch his satchel of notes. LucusAna crouches beside him and puts his hand on one of the young scholar's own. "Anphra, it's me, LucusAna." After a long moment AnphraJon uncurls a little. When he opens his eyes LucusAna says, "Thank you."

"I did nothing," AnphraJon whispers.

"You most certainly did. When you called out, your warning saved me. Most likely it saved us all."

AnphraJon shudders, then unfolds more. "I can't stop seeing it. I don't want to, but I can't. Will it ever stop?"

LucusAna doesn't know. Some part of him is harder now, in the same way his broken and mended arm is stronger than before. Yet AnphraJon is neither soft nor weak, it is more that he has a gentle soul and witnessing such violence has hurt him more than actual wounds. LucusAna envies that gentleness and hopes AnphraJon will not change. "Yes, it will, given time." It is only half a lie. "Come, let's see what they are talking about."

It is the right thing to say, AnphraJon cannot resist new knowledge, facts, truth, the reality of even unpleasant things.

Unlike most Aganathans he has chosen glyphs of thought and philosophy to be carved on his side-plates instead of the usual credo.

"Ah, there you are." MakuraMazara greets LucusAna warmly. "Here is one of the brave who stood tall beyond the walls when we confronted Osedax and turned them back."

A murmur of approval spreads through the gathered warriors and priests. LucusAna demurs, AnphraJon looms attentively behind.

"We were talking of survival and the future," MakuraMazara tells him, and LucusAna, who has feared some principled but doomed final stand is vastly relieved. "For that to become reality we must escape, and to escape we will need you and your godsteel."

Right now doing anything is better than thinking. "Tell me what to do."

MakuraMazara describes the plan: to carve a passage through the floor, out under the city to the wall, and beyond. Then, to avoid pursuit, to collapse the temple behind them.

"We c-cannot," LucusAna stammers. "The temple, Ro, they are one."

"Ro will not mind. They know we cannot take their symbol with us. Because we protect their mystery, they will protect us." MakuraMazara touches LucusAna's shoulder. "They will travel with us."

LucusAna can only hope she is right.

"Meanwhile, we hold here. The walls may be a body-length thick, but godflesh can be cut. We must watch for a breach at any point."

"That sounds like a job for me," a cheerful voice exclaims. It is CharAncho, LucusAna's great friend, bloody, happy, and marching towards them.

The general mood, determined if dour, improves notice-
ably, for CharAncho is a bit of a legend.

"Then it is yours. Pick your squad." MakuraMazara hesitates. "Was there anyone behind you? Anyone at all."

CharAncho waits until she has everyone's attention. "I was
the last, I swear."

MakuraMazara's arms hang limp at her sides. Then she
gathers herself. "Seal the doors. We are those who remain,
and we shall endure."

A great bustle ensues as people rush to do her bidding.
LucusAna goes to his friend.

"Cho, it is good to see you."

CharAncho takes in LucusAna's glued and repaired arm.
"I see you have had some fun."

LucusAna shudders. "I saw GalaTheo. We fought."

"You killed him?"

"He ran away."

"Ha. Myxini coward. Though they will fight if you give
them no choice." CharAncho looks deeply satisfied. "Most die
hard."

Down in the pit a few devout struggle against the weight
of Ro's great egg, wanting to push it around a final circuit. As
hard to start moving as it is to stop, it rolls silent and ponderous, a metaphor LucusAna has pondered more than once.
They watch them in silence.

"It is good so many Aganathan made it here," CharAncho
says. "You too, LucusAna. You too."

She leaves him abruptly, and heads towards the guards at
the main door, who greet her with noisy salutes and weapons
held high.

Doubt gnaws LucusAna like a worm in bone.
MakuraMazara calls him to her side. After consulting a large

diagram held by AnphraJon, she walks towards the rear wall and sketches a shape on the floor. "Cut here, and along here."

The upper layers of godflesh floor are hard and dry, compressed by generations of feet. LucusAna scores the outline of a rectangle as wide as his own body and twice as long. Then he leans his weight on his blade and cuts deeper. The floor resists the godsteel then parts and the blade sinks deep. LucusAna slices along his score marks on all four sides then steps back to let others peel back the hardened flesh.

MakuraMazara reaches down into the shallow excavation, pares away a slice of godflesh and eats it.

"It is sweet," she declares. "Strong and pure. This is a good sign, an omen of Ro's approval."

LucusAna leads the way, cutting crude chunks, then steps, down under the temple floor. Others haul out the spoil with long-handled gaffs and sharp-edged spades.

The godsteel does not blunt as even black godbone will. LucusAna is soon deep under the temple, cutting, slicing, finding his rhythm, stepping out for the spade work, then cutting again.

Ten feet down the meat turns to the deep layer of dense, pale godfat that lies between flesh and skin. It is a rich and rare treat for it has been consumed everywhere above ground generations past. LucusAna cannot resist. A spiced tingle fills his mouth, flavours he cannot fully describe, musty yet filled with life. A warmth spreads in his belly, strength fills his limbs.

"A gift from Ro," one of the other delvers says. "We head in the right direction."

Later, LucusAna comes across one of the great bones of the city, broad as his own body, slick and glistening, running alongside the tunnel he is cutting. As he works, there is sudden, startling movement and he cries out.

"What is it," one of the spade-workers calls down.

"Bone-worm!"

Everyone crowds in to look. It is a small one and soon retreats into the finger-width burrow it has bored. Anphra-Jon comes down, his bulk filling the tunnel. He measures the hole, width and depth, and records his findings.

Word spreads to those above, their disquiet feeds back down to the tunnel crew. Despite their promise Osedax has not waited, the Bone Clan army is already inside the city. Larval worm here, deep in the city's under-bones, proves they infest the entire skeleton. Within fifty cycles it will fail.

The tunnellers hang the livelight cages MakuraMazara sends down from hooks screwed into the tunnel roof. Weary as he is, LucusAna presses on with renewed urgency.

#

For two full cycles the victorious Myxini are content to leave the surviving Aganathans in their temple while they enjoy complete control of the rest of the city. LucusAna knows this control is an illusion. It does not matter that Albicaud, the Myxini pontiff, is determined to fight for his home, Osedax's army already burrows and grows inside the great bones of the city, it is already doomed.

He thinks about his former friend, GalaTheo, and discovers his love has turned to cold dislike.

"I don't hate him," he tells AnphraJon as he tries to work through his own feelings.

"No-one would blame you if you did. He tried to kill you."

This helps. LucusAna realises something, "He's not worthy of my hate."

"That's a good way of looking at it."

AnphraJon has such a calm nature LucusAna finds he can talk with him about things he would never discus with anyone else. "What about you? Is there anything you hate?"

"Oh, yes, several things," AnphraJon says without heat. He sees he has surprised LucusAna and quietly laughs.

While LucusAna works the Myxini slowly invest the temple. CharAncho prowls the walls with her guards, stopping now and then to press a listening bell against the godflesh wall. "Let them come," she proclaims. "We are ready."

"What are they doing out there?" MakuraMazara asks. "Can you tell?"

"Scratching and scrapping." CharAncho lifts her tail high, vibrating. "They are scared." Her guards copy her and clatter their spears and poles against their bodies.

"We're eighteen lengths along," LucusAna reports to the vice-philosopher. "AnphraJon calculates we are just outside the temple."

MakuraMazara consults her diagrams and agrees. "Ten more lengths to reach beyond the city wall. How long?"

Down in the tunnel everyone has been living on godfat. LucusAna feels stronger and healthier than he has done since he was second moult. "One cycle."

"Come to me again when you reach godskin." MakuraMazara takes both his first hands in her own. "You have served the Aganathans well. Eternal Ro is well pleased." Suddenly all attention is on LucusAna.

In a sudden outburst CharAncho flourishes her godsteel and shouts, "I say we cut a sally-port and take the fight to them!"

"Won't that give them a way in?" AnphraJon says.

"Numbers count for nothing when you are in the right."

AnphraJon stares at CharAncho like she is some kind of fool. "Numbers always count," he tells LucusAna later. "I think she is jealous."

While LucusAna and his team delve onwards, other teams prepare to collapse the temple. Now the decision has been made, there is a strangely gleeful enthusiasm. Guided by AnphraJon, volunteers cut most of the way through the supporting pillars, lash sinew ropes around them and run them back to the escape tunnel.

Meanwhile, the scratching and scraping continues all along the wall that runs beside Great Heart Road. AnphraJon borrows the listening bell and works his way slowly along the wall, listening high and low. When he is done, he hurries back to MakuraMazara.

"They are going as quietly as they can, but they are cutting away the entire wall left of the main door."

"Nonsense," CharAncho says. "How can you say this?"

Once again AnphraJon stares CharAncho down. "Because I once tried such a thing with my apprentices and listened with this very bell. I know the sounds."

MakuraMazara is impressed, but CharAncho tosses her head. "Say they are, then what?"

"Then they push."

"So? We push back."

"Then they wind in bone screws and pull. It achieves nothing."

"I say not. We must attack!" CharAncho exclaims. "Drive them back in blood and confusion."

MakuraMazara gives a deep, thoughtful exhalation. "AnphraJon, what would you do?"

"If we block immediately, they pull. Blocking buys almost no time," AnphraJon says.

"So we just let them come? We will be over-run!"

"Almost. If block a body-length back they are committed. The gaps at each end will be narrow, we can hold them there. If they want to pull, they must completely withdraw." AnphraJon faces CharAncho and bows. "Attack then, if you will. That will buy even more time."

CharAncho's mandibles chew air. "You claim to know a lot about war, you who have never fought, or held so much as a sharp stick."

MakuraMazara steps between them. "CharAncho, this will be our plan. Build a stop for the wall, heavy and deep. Act quickly. Take who and what you need."

"They are through!" A shout of alarm comes from the guards at the wall. Godsteel glitters under the glimmering livelights as a blade tips emerge from the outer wall, and withdraws.

A wave of fear close to terror pulses through the Aganathan families sheltering in the temple.

Far down along the tunnel LucusAna feels the ripple of panic. After cycles of work they have reached a vertical wall of godfat, the city skin is an arm's length away. He cuts with renewed urgency, the spade team slice and lift away rectangular hunks of fat until the purple-black of the city's godskin is revealed.

Only a finger length thick, the godskin is so hard LucusAna finds it slow-going even with his steel. Then he is through, and small trickle of grey silt oozes through the cut. Sheathing his blade, he hurries back down the tunnel under swaying livelight cages.

Up in the temple order is sliding towards chaos. A circle of armed guards now surrounds the top of the steps down to the tunnel, holding back a noisy press of family groups. Males have formed into belligerent gangs, females hold up their children like offerings.

"They are through, the Myxini!" AnphraJon hurries LucusAna over to the outer wall and shows him the now complete cuts along half its length. Godbone spars have been set into holes cut into the floor back from the wall, holes filled with glue that is only half-set. Pilled behind the spars is an enormous weight of godmeat.

CharAncho struts from one side to the other with her warrior band, her tail held so high it curves over her body.

"This is where we stand," she proclaims as she flourishes her blade. "Not one step back. I will stand here, I will fight here. I will win or I will die. Are you with me?"

The response is wild and immediate. LucusAna has never seen such an eagerness for blood and death and sacrifice.

MakuraMazara rushes up to him, dishevelled and frantic. "Tell me you have reached the wall. Tell me we are ready to go."

LucusAna feels the weight of history upon him as he says, "I have cut the godskin. A small job now to make a larger opening."

"Thank the good gods." MakuraMazara grips his shoulders. "Go, now, LucusAna, finish your work."

Never has LucusAna felt more wanted, more part of the community that took him in. "I shall."

In his absence the spade team have enlarged his small cut, opening a flap in the godskin down both sides and across the base, leaving the top edge attached. Blocks of muddy siltstone are piled along the edges of the tunnel. LucusAna lifts the godskin flap up into the excavated space and props it with bone spars and cross-pieces. It is a matter of moments to dig a ramp up through the siltstone. Spade-heads break into free space, a lid of soft stone collapses, dust billows, eager hands claw lumpy earth aside.

LucusAna clambers through. Behind him the city wall gleams, sleek, dark and sheer. He reaches down and helps his team out, one by one. They shake themselves and look around in awe. He shares the feeling, for although he has been outside the city before it was only the once. One by one they all look back down at the hole in the ground.

"It doesn't look like much, but we have saved everyone we know and love," LucusAna says.

The spade-team look to each other and LucusAna. He feels such a bond of kinship with these men and women, whose names he is still learning. He I sure it is something that will last forever.

"Go back and tell them," one of them says. "Bring them through."

LucusAna ducks back down and returns quickly. "They are already coming."

#

The Aganathans pour from the tunnel in a steady column and spread across the grey plain beneath the city wall. Everyone brings with them as much godflesh or godfat as they can carry. A mass of family groups and individuals lead the way, a score of militia herd a straggle of solitary children who clutch their own hands and look around. Last of all come MakuraMazara and the Aganathan priesthood. Somehow, with their pennants and banners held high, they bring a sense of dignity and direction to what in reality is headlong flight.

Half the adults cower under the infinite, dark sky, even militia and priests-militant, though children of first and second moult take it all in their stride. Some comfort their elders, the rest look around in wonder. Here is vast new experience, a new life, perhaps adventure.

But here and there are those who cover their eyes and mutter and rock, it is too much for them. Some rush back into the tunnel, a handful of others bound away across the grey plain shrieking. No one tries to stop them.

For a while chaos threatens as hysteria spreads.

"Anyone who can, help me," MakuraMazara says. Those with experience, like LucusAna, or with harder heads like RingenZaem, form a stable core. Along with the older children they comfort the distressed and isolate the truly manic. Order is slowly restored.

The vice-philosopher calls two priest together and climbs onto their backs. Another hands her a pennant bearing a white circle. "We are all outcasts and refugees now, orphans of our own city. We Aganathans have always taken in the abandoned and alone." As she says this she dips her head towards LucusAna, who acknowledges the truth of her words. "Here and now let us not forget our own orphaned children."

She speaks to good effect, for all those solitary children, the first, second, and even third moult, are taken into one or other of the family groups.

LucusAna senses huge movement behind him and turns to see the city wall quiver, ripple, then sag back into a great fold. Whoever remains in Ro's great temple has collapsed the pillars.

A steady wind begins to blow from the escape tunnel, stronger and stronger. Small flecks of godflesh gust out, then larger chunks. Driven by the roof sinking like a great bellows, the wind grows so strong nobody can stand in its path. The, suddenly, it stops.

CharAncho and three priests-militant burst from the tunnel like bungs from a bladder, propelled by a disgusting spew of blood, macerated flesh and organs. Propelled through the air, CharAncho rolls once then stands. She is caked in, and dripping, gore. Her secondary right arm is off at the elbow, one of her left-side legs is dislocated. Nevertheless, she turns and tries to rush back into the tunnel.

It is futile. The tunnel is flattened by the weight of the fallen roof and wall. Nobody else will escape the temple.

Wild livelights swarm over and around the Aganathans, feeding on the blood mist and drifting specks of flesh. Under their swirling multi-point glow LucusAna helps CharAncho stand. The same surgeon who mended his arm quickly attends her, cleaning and sealing her elbow stump while she hisses and frets.

"This hurts." The surgeon braces himself against CharAncho's body, pulls hard on her dislocated leg, twists, and eases it back onto its socket. CharAncho's mouth sags, her eyes phase white. Then she is back. She tests her leg and find it tender, but sound.

"I deserve this. The pain. Everything," CharAncho says dully. "My arrogant pride."

LucusAna tries to comfort her "You did what you could. Nobody could have done more."

"Yes, I could. I could... down through the years. So much more. The Myxini paid, but not enough." Her head hangs. "I thought it was a game."

Close behind them one of the three priests-militant clears his throat, and again, then collapses onto one side and expires.

CharAncho utters a broken wail of frustration and rage.

Traumatised by her first true defeat, LucusAna has never seen his friend like this. He feels profound pity for her, for she has finally discovered what everyone else has always known—a warrior's life is not some happy game.

MakuraMazara consults with AnphraJon, then leads them away from the city across the grey plain. Priests, guards, adults and children, nine hundred souls are all that remain of the Aganathan sect. All are exhausted, many are hurt, some are truly broken and their minds may never fully mend. Everyone needs rest. Nevertheless, burdened as they are by great hunks of godflesh, the trauma of expulsion and the sights they have seen, they must put distance between themselves and the triumphant Myxini.

They march for half a cycle. Behind them, the dark hump of the city falls back into distant gloom. In all directions the undulating grey plain rolls away to vision's limit. A vast distance away past their left shoulder a broken line of baleful red light fitfully glimmers. Overhead, above the pulsing bells of occasional swarms of wild livelights, the empty sky stretches to an unguessable height, a dark infinity.

It is too much for some and they fall by the wayside. Bolstered by his godfat diet, LucusAna is stronger than most. He and the other diggers help them back to their feet and walk with them, they let first moult children climb onto their backs. Thanks to them, nobody is left behind.

A line on the ground cuts across their path. MakuraMazara leads them towards it confidently. To his absolute astonishment LucusAna sees it is a paved surface, a road eight and ten body lengths wide, raised half a span above the surface of the endless mudstone.

They climb onto it and stop to rest. Fascinated and amazed, LucusAna walks a short distance. The road is constructed from rectangular grey-green blocks a handspan wide and twice as long, set in a simple interlocked pattern. Here and there silt has drifted across the edge and the very fact that it has, in this timeless changeless place, tells him that the road is astonishingly old. Who built it, he wonders. And why?

"We don't know," AnphraJon tells him. "All we know is its name. This is the God Road."

2. The God Road

MakuraMazara consults with AnphraJon, who takes his notes from his satchel, reads, and looks about, and reads again. He looks across to the far line of red light and back towards the city, then points down the road in the direction that leads away from them both.

Everyone rests and eats. LucusAna is not hungry. He thinks about this, then cuts the mass of godfat he carries into two, trades one half for twice as much godflesh and packs it away.

MakuraMazara comes to him and holds out her hand. "May I see that fine blade you carry?"

LucusAna senses something is not quite right and takes a step back. "Why?"

Two priests-militant stand at MakuraMazara's shoulder, cringing slightly under the sky. CharAncho lurks in the background. The vice-philosopher says, "LucusAna, as a child we took you in, we gave you the best of starts, sheltering and feeding you just as the city sheltered and fed us. But the city is gone and this is where our paths diverge. You hold Aganathan godsteel and I ask for its return."

It feels like the ground has been cut out from under his feet. LucusAna can think of nothing to say. "You... You gave it to me."

"A new city has fallen along the god road. That is where Aganathan destiny now lies." MakuraMazara spreads all her hands. "And all things considered, you are not Aganathan."

"I— I am."

"No, child." MakuraMazara speaks slowly, as if explaining an obvious thing to a simple person. "No, you are not. You are merely adopted." She beckons again. "Now, the sword."

LucusAna's mind seethes. He fought the Myxini, he carved out the temple tunnel, many Aganathans would be dead if not for him. He has lived his entire life from second moult as an Aganathan. Aganathan philosophy is carved on the edge-plates of his body.

His confusion morphs to inchoate anger. He sees now that MakuraMazara's words are hollow. She has used him.

Great as that anger is, it is as nothing compared to the hurt he feels, his afront at her sheer entitlement. Who is she to say who believes? He believes! His tail rises, his side-plates rattle. She gifted him the godsteel. He takes the blade in a two-handed grip. "No. It is mine."

By now many people are watching. MakuraMazara looks left and right and waves the priests-militant forward. Two more join them, then another.

LucusAna is frightened. "CharAncho!"

His best and oldest friend, the one person with whom he as ever shared moult-feast, will not meet his eye. "I am Aganathan, I must follow... I cannot fail my people... Not again." She takes a step back, and then another, and LucusAna's heart breaks.

Away to one side RingenZaem makes a sound of sheer disgust. She pushes through the priests-militant and stands beside LucusAna. "LucusAna kept my tail safe when we fought the Myxini mob. I say he has earned the right to keep his steel, and his place among us."

One by one her squad come across. Outnumbered, the priests militant do not move.

MakuraMazara turns to CharAncho and RingenZaem laughs derisively. "Don't expect that one to start a fight she knows she cannot win. Come on, draw your blade, CharAncho, my godbone against your steel. It will be my pleasure. Let us see who strikes the mortal blow."

CharAncho does something LucusAna has never seen her do before. She hesitates.

Voices come from the crowd:

"Let him stay."

"Aganathans should not fight each another."

"Let him keep it."

A long moment passes during which MakuraMazara neither speaks nor moves. Then she gives an exaggerated shrug. "I am persuaded." She turns away and calls back over her shoulder with feigned indifference. "Keep it as a life-gift."

RingenZaem loiters beside LucusAna until the vice-philosopher is out of earshot. "Take care with that offer, it is insincere."

LucusAna knows what she means. Life-gifts revert to the donor on death. Accidents happen even in the safest places, and neither the journey to the new city nor the city itself will be that. A sour taste fills his mouth, suddenly he is so angry his body plates lock solid. When RingenZaem speaks it as if she has read his mind.

"I am sick of this hypocrisy. What do you want to do?"

"You mean...?"

"I mean I'm with you." RingenZaem says. "Myxini creed, Aganathan philosophy, what's the point of any of it if all we do is squabble over cutlery?"

LucusAna laughs, and despite everything a weight lifts, the sourness has gone. "It's more a case of what I don't want to do, and what I can't do. What has been denied me."

RingenZaem calls her squad together. Unlike the priests-militant and other warrior groups their discipline is solid. If being under the limitless sky bothers them it does not show.

"As of this moment we choose our own paths. Oaths you once made, I release you from. Stay as friends, or return to the Aganathans. They will need help staking a claim in the new city. Nobody will hold it against you that you once stood oathbound with me."

Only two decide to stay. Then, reluctant but decided, with many protestations of friendship and bonds never to be forgotten, the rest depart.

LucusAna takes stock. They have food for many cycles, steel and bone, and the strength of their bodies. As he ponders the future AnphraJon joins them.

"Where are you going?"

In all honesty, LucusAna has not got that far. "Not back to the old city, or to the new." He looks down the god road in the other direction.

"I've already lived in a city, so if you are thinking of going over to that line of red light I will join you," AnphraJon says.

"What is it?"

"I have no idea."

A fatalistic mood comes over LucusAna. "Why not?"

"Who is this big fellow," RingenZaem enquires politely.

"AnphraJon, the scholar. He stood with us when we fought the mob."

"Ah, I remember now. The one who did not fight."

"Nobody knows more of the wider world than Anphra-Jon."

"There is not much that is known," AnphraJon admits, "But what there is, I know it all."

RingenZaem introduces her two erstwhile squad members, ThunusMunid and HarlDranath. By all appearances they are capable and serious folk, yet here they are, having chosen to be outcasts from the outcasts.

"Zaem will look after us," ThunusMunid says. "Anyway, city life became predictable. Kill, fight, kill."

HarlDranath agrees. "Fight, kill, fight."

They laugh and share a wild look. LucusAna realises they are final moult and bonded. Where one goes, the other will always follow.

"Five of us, then," LucusAna says. Three warriors, LucusAna himself, and half as big again as any of them, young AnphraJon.

They are ready, there is nothing to keep them. LucusAna will not look back.

The god road is easy to walk and the miles pass by. AnphraJon updates his notes as they go. "It's strange, I never even thought why we needed units of length so large as miles and leagues when I lived in the city."

None of the others had heard of such measures and AnphraJon explains the system, though only LucusAna is really interested.

"It sounds complicated," HarlDranath says.

"Useful. Out here I can see it is useful. Except..."

"Except what?" LucusAna says.

"Some of these old measures are so extravagant it's ludicrous. How does it help to know how far light travels in a year?"

Now even RingenZaem is interested. "Light moves?"

"Incredibly fast. Faster than sound, faster than anything at all."

"And what is a year?"

AnphraJon admits he does not know.

It's not long before LucusAna feels the beginnings of an old familiar itch. His diet of godfat while tunnelling has accelerated his body towards moult time. The itch spreads to his plate joints and knees, but this time his excitement and anticipation of coming relief is overwhelmed by anxiety.

There is no shelter, he barely knows his companions. His trepidation grows until he can barely think for anxiety. In the end there is nothing for it.

"I'm going into moult," he confesses.

"Oh, great. Perfect timing," HarlDranath says.

"Come on, it is what it is," ThunusMunid chides.

"Yes, all right. Sorry." HarlDranath dips his head in apology. "Sorry, LucusAna."

"It's 'Ana,'" LucusAna says, and finds he likes the feeling his words bring. "My friends call me Ana."

"Harl, then."

"Final moult?" AnphraJon says.

"I'm not sure." Normally, yes, but there's all the godfat he's eaten. It's entirely possible he'll have an intervening moult. He tells himself that now CharAncho is gone, now the one person he had dared dream to bond with has left, perhaps this is a good thing.

It doesn't feel like a good thing.

"All right," RingenZaem says. "First, congratulations. I'm glad for you, we all are, but we need to find shelter. How long, do you think until-?"

"A cycle, two at most."

HarlDranath rolls his eyes and laughs.

Back in the city moult was never a problem. The city *was* the shelter, the livelights could be controlled, there would be a room for him in one of Ro's temples, safe and quiet. CharAncho would stand guard...

These thoughts are not helpful.

RingenZaem says, "There's nothing here. Let's push on."

Miles turn to leagues. Although the glimmering, leaping wall of red light ahead does not appear to come any closer they can now see that vast plumes of black smoke boil above it. All around them the mudstone plain begins to wrinkle, then lift into parallel folds of increasing height. Another league and the ground shrugs off the mudstone and thrusts up into sharp-peaked ridges of a bedrock none of them have seen before, greenish-black and flecked with tiny translucent fragments.

"This would be a useful material," AnphraJon says. "If we could work it."

It must be possible, for the god road continues onwards, flat and level, cutting through the upthrusts of the new rock.

HarlDranath points with his spear. "Over there. A light."

#

A narrow path breaks from the god road and runs into one of the rock-fold valleys. Surfaced with smooth mudstone, it winds away between smaller upthrusts of base rock. Any loose stones have been carefully pushed aside. Clearly it is a made thing. They go single file, it is easy walking.

Half a mile in, set under a long overhang where the green-black stone seems to have melted and folded up and back, are a series of cave mouths. The smallest lies at the near end, the largest at the far. In the mouth of that largest cave hangs an ornate lantern of livelights.

"Who would choose to live here?" LucusAna wonders aloud. "An explorer, a hermit?"

"Who can say,?" RingenZaem says, then calls out. "Haloo! Travellers passing through."

When there is no reply HarlDranath pushes to the front, spear at the ready. "Let's take a look."

Even though it is the largest cave there is only room for one to enter at a time. HarlDranath takes one step inside, spear forward and tail high. After a moment he calls back:

"It's empty. No, there's something at the back." He goes further in. As he does, his tail brushes the hanging lantern. "This cave is strange. And those aren't livelights, the whole lantern glows. It's like it's part of the roof, a growth." He reaches up, prods the lantern and sets it swaying.

Outside, LucusAna sees a row of eight small black eyes blink open across the top of the cave mouth. A moment of terrible realisation dawns. "Get out!" he screams. "Get out now!"

"What's the matter?" HarlDranath begins to turn. Then, with a shuddering quiver, the cave mouth snaps shut.

"Harl!" ThunusMunid flings herself forwards and batters wildly at the rock-like face of the creature with her godbone knife. "Harl. Harl!"

Up above, beyond her reach, eight eyes look down, turn in different directions, then close behind stony lids.

The creature's mouth has shut down to ground level. ThunusMunid grips the stony lip and tries to lift it. "Help me!"

No matter how hard the four of them try, they cannot prise the mouth open. Its skin is hard, blocky, and impervious to the blows of godbone. Almost perfectly like the surrounding stone, they can only see it for what it is because they know it is there.

"Let me try." LucusAna swings and cuts with his godsteel to little effect. He pushes the tip into a crack between the blocks of armoured skin and is rewarded by a spurt of dense reddish-brown liquid. He leans on the blade and pushes hard. Blood spurts, the creature shudders and suddenly pulls back, threatening to snatch the weapon from his grip.

"Cut it again," ThunusMunid cries. "Cut it open."

LucusAna readies himself, but before he can move the creature surges forwards, bowling him over and scattering the others.

Free of the cave it scurries out on four spindly multi-jointed legs, an ungainly box-shaped creature with a stubby fan-tail. It raises a low spined crest, double-hinged wing-fins unfold from its side, strutted with fingers of bone. Before any of them can regain their feet it crouches, leaps, and batters its way up into the sky, wing-fins clapping together at the top of each beat. Within moments it is gone.

For a long while ThunusMunid is inconsolable. Turning in circles, she flings rocks at the sky, at anyone who comes close. Eventually she is physically and emotionally exhausted and sinks into a fugue of despair. Left alone, she would never recover. RingenZaem and AnphraJon embrace her, take her hands, soothe her with quiet words and softer sounds. Slowly, they bring her back, then hold her as she howls and shudders.

LucusAna wants to comfort her but the imperatives from his incipient moult demand otherwise. He feels too big for his size, his limbs ache, his body feels stiff and bloated. And also, why should he trust her?

In a sudden separation, his belly-plates slither and he feels afraid and vulnerable. He needs shelter. Overhead the sky is vast and terrible, an all-seeing eye. His need to hide is overwhelming, the cave the creature abandoned irresistible. Consumed with guilt and need, he backs into it and watches his three companions, a tight-knit group of comforting, murmuring embrace.

A strange mood creeps up on him and he becomes convinced that discussing him. Perhaps ThunusMunid is only pretending grief and they plan some dark conspiracy. It is likely and, after all, he barely knows them. LucusAna laughs quietly, he is not so weak, he wields godsteel. Let them come.

RingenZaem looks at him, breaks away and comes over. "Never fear, we'll protect you during moult."

Even though part of him knows this is moult-madness, LucusAna fears RingenZaem standing so close. "Keep back. You can do that over there."

"Of course." RingenZaem holds up her hands and backs away. Convinced her reply was too glib, LucusAna withdraws deeper into the cave.

Yet he needs their help. It's not long before wild livelights begin to gather, first in twos and threes, then by dozens. Undefended, they would slip under his loosening carapace to probe and sip at his soft insides, to lay eggs. He feels something on his back. Terrified they are already feeding on him, he grinds his back on the cave roof.

Outside, ThunusMunid drives away the livelights in a frenzy of anger. RingenZaem and AnphraJon deal with things neither of them have seen before. Many-legged segmented creatures with black-bead eyes and jointed antennae crawl over the valley edge from the direction of the line of red light. Mock-children, their undifferentiated bodies and limbs are unsettlingly like first-moult juveniles.

Other creatures with vertically compressed bodies the colour of stone emerge from cracks in the rock. Using their tightly curved tails, they flip themselves forwards in unpredictable tumbling jumps. Everyone has their work cut out.

RingenZaem runs to the cave. "LucusAna, we need your blade." LucusAna shrieks in terror, convinced she intends mischief.

"We're not going to hurt you." She tosses her own god-bone weapon towards him and points back to the growing mass of scavengers and livelights, "But those things will."

LucusAna scuttles forward and snatches up her bone blade. "Haha! Foolish. Come closer and I will kill you, I will kill you all."

RingenZaem hisses with impatience and rushes into the cave. She pins LucusAna's first arms against the walls with her own weight. "Now, Anphra."

AnphraJon may not know how to fight, but he is strong. LucusAna struggles, spits, and curses, but cannot stop him from prising his fingers open and taking the godsteel blade.

"Got it."

RingenZaem is soon causing havoc with the godsteel. LucusAna glares at them from the cave mouth, clutching the godbone spear she left him.

He feels his side-plates split with a near overwhelming mix of relief, fear, and pain. Unable to help himself, he cries out. Wriggling and shuffling, he enlarges the tear, then pulls his legs on his left side free of their old casing. He treads down with feet that feel too soft, too flexible, and extracts his right-side limbs. He works his tail free. He pulls open his thorax, and oh, the intensity of fear and delight, and backs out of his old body. His shoulders come, his arms, his hands, his soft and pliable fingers. The relief of freedom vies with fear of vulnerability. Instinctively he gulps, again and again, and his body swells. His heart thumps, his segments pulse, his tail vanes expand. Only his old head case remains.

Outside, RingenZaem cuts and kills the scavengers and their blood and flesh become a distraction for the rest. Crabs feast on their dead kin, livelights drop to join them. The narrow black creatures grasp hunks of dead flesh and spring back to their crevice lairs.

LucusAna takes hold of the collar of old segments at his neck, closes his eyes, and pulls his old head case down over his face. Jaw and mouth parts go with them, new ones flop below. Temporarily he cannot speak or eat.

He lies exhausted but fulfilled, free of his old self. He is soft, he is easy prey, he is filled with the ecstasy that follows the departure of the right kind of pain. Slowly the pulsing in his segments abates, his new carapace begins to harden. He moves carefully, knowing he will be clumsy until he adjusts to his larger size, and that any damage inflicted now will be permanent. He looks out of the cave with a new clarity. AnphraJon raises a hand. He, RingenZaem, even ThunusMunid, have kept their promise and kept LucusAna is safe. As his mind clears of moult-madness he feels shamed to have doubted them. They are his friends. He tries to apologise but his mouth is too soft and all he manages is an incoherent mumble. Exhaustion claims him and he sleeps.

When LucusAna wakes his moult is complete, each segment hard and strong. He feels refreshed, almost purified, deeply comfortable in his new form. He flexes his limbs, his hands, works his mouth and inspects his body. The repairs to his broken arm and the places the surgeon cut splints from his body are replaced by good new carapace, smooth, and unsullied.

Gone too are the quotations from Aganathan credo carved onto his side plates. He decides he will not miss them.

He emerges from the cave and finds his three companions gathered in a circle, feasting on mock-children and the narrow-bodied black-shelled things. Feeling more than a little ashamed he goes over to them. ThunusMunid moves aside to make space, RingenZaem silently hands him his godsteel and he returns her bone blade. AnphraJon proffers a handful of meat, striated pink and white. "It's good, sweet."

"Thank you." LucusAna takes it and eats. "Thank you, one and all."

The mood is fragile. HarlDranath's death followed so quickly by his own moult-madness has nearly broken them as a group. One wrong word or deed will shatter them completely. There is only one thing he can think to do.

LucusAna returns to the cave and breaks four small side-plates from his old carapace, now a translucent gold-brown thing. On the cusp of the moment he hesitates, for he has done this once before and it ended in heartbreak. *I will do it,* he decides. *For us all. For me.*

He carries them outside and waits for everyone's attention. When he has it, he hands out three of the pieces. "This is part of me. Let us be together, let us be as one."

It is an old, old ritual.

ThunusMunid looks at the piece she holds long enough for LucusAna to worry she will reject it. Then she lifts it to her mouth and eats. Slowly, solemnly the others follow.

Carapace has a taste like no other—smoky, dense, lived-in.

"We are as one," RingenZaem speaks with sincerity. "I am honoured beyond compare."

AnphraJon opens and closes his mouth several times. "I have never... Nobody ever before asked me... I..."

LucusAna touches his shoulder and AnphraJon clasps his hand. "Let us be as one."

"My good new friend," LucusAna says to ThunusMunid. "I am so sorry I could not be with you when you needed me most."

She nods once and keeps her head lowered. "Bad timing." Then she straightens her shoulders. "I hold Harl's seed in my body. When my eggs are ripe he will live again."

"I am glad," LucusAna says, and discovers he is, very much.

ThunusMunid eats again, leans forward and bumps her brow against his own. "We are as one."

"Now and ever."

He can hope.

#

The last remnants of the Aganathan tribe set out along the god road towards where MakuraMazara's scouts assure them the new godfall lies. They now number something over eight hundred and cycle by cycle, by ones and twos, that number reduces. Flocks of wild livelights weaken already weakening stragglers, mole crab pits await the unwary.

It is not until three full cycles have passed, during which fifteen adults and three children have died, or in three cases simply disappeared, that the vice-philosopher accepts her scouts advice to set guards when the main group rests.

"Something is coming into your camp," One of them tells her.

"What is it?"

"Something new to us."

"Then find out."

"Find out yourself."

The vice-philosopher is not used to being spoken to that way. Before she can retort the scout is gone. She is angry, but anger will not help. Where is the respect? Not for herself, she is well aware she has made mistakes, but for her rank. Out here the hierarchies of the city are all that keep them together.

CharAncho has witnessed the encounter. The scout has a natural confidence, a self-possession CharAncho feels she has lost. It exerts a powerful draw and she follows the scout back to their own camp, a small enclave separate from the main group.

She comes close, limping slightly, for her leg is still tender, and makes the sign, the Aganathan weave. "May I join you?"

Sitting in a circle, none of the scouts return the sign, but one of them casually waves her forward.

She comes closer and still most ignore her. She realises they are waiting for her to say what she wants. "I am CharAncho."

"I've heard that name," one of them says. He is lightly built, like all scouts his carapace has a dark hue. The only thing that marks him as Aganathan is the style of their godskin harness. Instead of Aganathan inscriptions, the side plates of his carapace are covered in scores of small punch-dots.

"I wondered if I might sit here with you a while."

"We are resting."

After a moment CharAncho realises that this is their way of saying they have time for her. Feeling like a third-moult adolescent in the presence of adults, she asks her questions and has them answered.

Each punch dot represents a cycle lived outside the city.

Since third moult none of them have lived inside.

New scouts are not recruited, they are declared.

They ask about how she lost her arm; about godsteel; about the last days in the city. CharAncho does her best to tell the plain truth without adornment or swagger. She admits her mistakes.

"It seems you have shown great resilience," AmkaTan, the scout who first spoke to her says.

"Thank you." She finds his praise means more than anything MakuraMazara ever said. The insight startles her. All her life she has been praised, often it has approached adulation and her desire for more drove her behaviour. Looking back she realises such acclaim was only because she was useful within some larger agenda. Her friends have been few enough, and only LucusAna-

They were bonded, as one, and it was her who broke them in two. Guilt wells up inside her, and deep shame. Only LucusAna. She knows she will never see him again. She knows she is strong and courageous, it was the praise made her arrogant. She did the right things for the wrong reasons. LucusAna appears unbidden in her mind and she knows she did the wrong things for the wrong reasons as well. Ringen-Zaem saw right through her.

In a surge of self-hatred CharAncho decides she no longer wants to be the person she has been. Scouts, she has been told, are declared. She takes a breath and speaks humbly.

"I would be a scout. Though I am ignorant of the most basic skills."

All the scouts look her over. "Ay-ha," they say in unison. That is so.

AmkaTan looks her up and down. "So, then. Godsteel."

Thinking he wants the weapon, CharAncho draws the weapon and offers it to him. "As far as I know, if it lives, this blade will cut it."

"The life of a scout seldom involves warfare."

Believing she understands, CharAncho drops the priceless weapon onto the ground and feels free.

The scouts make a space for her in their circle. Somewhat overawed, she steps into it. Before she knows what he is doing, AmkaTan places a bone punch on her carapace and hits it with a stone. Her first cycle is marked.

"I will guide you," he says. "Now, pick up your weapon, for you are going to need it."

#

The god road heads into an increasingly rugged landscape of titanic bedrock folds. LucusAna marvels at the effort taken to keep the road level, the sheer ability to cut through what are now small mountains. Although it bends and curves back in slow meanders, it heads unerringly towards the line of red light. The wind is steady and always at their backs.

A full league from the light-line the mountains abruptly end and they emerge onto a rolling plain of bedrock. They see the red line is a fiery chasm cutting across their path. Sheets of flame twenty and thirty body-lengths high leap and die and leap again along its entire length as far as they can see. Black smoke plumes boil from clusters of towering stone vents scattered across the plain. The wind is stronger here, the smoke plumes all bend towards the fire line. Whatever lies on the far side is hidden by the towering flame-sheets, seething smoke, and the shimmering heat of the air.

LucusAna, who has never imagined anything like this, is awed by the sight. "Is there a way across?"

"I don't know," AnphraJon confesses. "There's nothing in the histories. If there was a way once..."

He doesn't need to say it. The god road is ancient.

AnphraJon lifts a foot and puts it down again, then stoops and places all his hands flat on the ground. "The ground is vibrating."

At the same time RingenZaem points across the wasteland. "Someone is coming."

A group of five people cuts down across the plain towards the god road. Even though they are still some distance off it is clear they are well-equipped, with spears and livelight cages. Large panniers hang from their body harnesses. They might be some roving Myxini or Aganathan war band, yet they carry no banners, and their close line seems defensive rather than militant.

"We should talk to them," AnphraJon says. "They might be from another city."

The rough plain all around them is open, without cover or advantage in any direction. RingenZaem loosens her god-bone blade. "They certainly seem to want to talk to us."

ThunusMunid draws her own weapon and growls. "Always happy to chat."

LucusAna wants to tell them to relax, that all encounters need not be mortal. Yet since he fought alongside Ringen-Zaem in the riots he cannot think of one that has not been bloody, or a betrayal, or a trap, so he too prepares for war.

It is AnphraJon who shows them a new kind of courage when he steps down off the road and walks towards the strangers.

The only thing he carries approaching a weapon is a small godbone knife for cutting food. He holds it high, in clear view, and puts it on the ground.

"Greetings."

One of the strangers hands their single-edged glaive to their companion and walks forwards, all hands open. A full body length from AnphraJon, they halt.

LucusAna and the others approach within listening distance.

"Well met, we hope." Their accent is strange, with a hard lilt. *Hwell mett, hwe houp.*

"Well met, I say this is true. Know that we are unaffiliated, neither Myxini nor Aganathan. However, we are open-minded and accord both ideals due respect."

The stranger tips their head. "These concepts are not familiar to us. Perhaps this is a good thing?"

AnphraJon bows. "It is. Shall we now sit, and talk and eat?"

"We shall."

He is Griem qa Jago and his companions are from the families Jago and Barabal. Their names, their accents, and that their carapaces are carved with intricate decorative knotwork instead of credo is more than enough to prove they come from a different place. They share steaks of squat lobster, a fibrous white meat, savoury and moist, and are delighted when LucusAna gifts them a heavy slab of godfat. Cautious friendliness grows as the two groups relax. They do not know each other at all. There is much to discuss.

"We quest for Rasteliger, the black-smoke smith," Griem says. "We hope to be of service and hope in return they will provide us with better weapons for our onward journey."

"We are outcasts from our city's fall," RingenZaem replies. "Our faction leader betrayed us, another group fights the bone worm clans."

Griem shakes his head. "Such idiocies led us to depart our own city many cycles past. Though we were only third and fourth moult we could still see the truth."

"Aya, and the lies," his companions say.

LucusAna is fascinated by them. They are all final moult and have lived outside their entire adult lives. They know much of the wider world.

"We met a creature..." he begins, then turns to ThunusMu-nid, who bows in silent permission to continue.

"We met a creature that looked like a cave lit by live-lights. One of us was..." The words form in his throat but he cannot say them.

"Lampmouths," Griem says. "We lost one of our own in the early days. Never since."

The admission draws the two groups together. Polite friendliness becomes more relaxed. Everyone has questions.

"This was the only thing that hurt it," LucusAna says. He draws his godsteel blade, and everything changes.

#

Despite setting guards another one of the Aganathans has disappeared during the rest period.

"They walked back along the road a way." MakuraMazara tells the scouts.

"Alone?"

The vice-philosopher sighs. "The guards thought it would be safe because we had just crossed that ground."

AmkaTan's look says it all.

CharAncho wants to prove herself in her new role as scout but is aware of her limits. She draws her blade. "I could take a look. If I see anything at all, I'll come straight back."

"Stay on the road," AmkaTan tells her.

She gives the priests-militant rearguard a slow look as she passes through them and they shuffle their feet.

The road is the road. Here and there silt has drifted across the raised edge. Here and there on each side are steep-sided conical pits dug by mole crabs. Only their slender jointed eye stalks are visible at the bottom. Off in the distance the warm glow of a lampmouth promise a deceptive refuge.

CharAncho walks carefully and slowly, scanning the road ahead, to the left, and the right. The road has been swept clean by the passage of several hundred Aganathans, the rectangular blocks are free of silt and debris. There are no tracks, no signs of disturbance. Here and there trails wind out onto the desolate mudstone plain and back again, created by scouts or guards flanking the main group or the simply curious. As far as she can tell every set of footprints returns to the road.

Something is out there, something inimical. People just don't disappear. Alert and cautious, CharAncho unconsciously grips her blade and walks ten more paces.

The god road folds away under her feet and she tumbles into a dark void. The fall is long, the ground hard. CharAncho lands on her back, her blade flies from her grasp, ringing against stone. For a moment she lies stunned.

Something large and multi-legged rustles in the gloom. Overhead the section of road swings up and closes. Utter darkness descends.

"Rejoice." The whisper word is filled with odd clicks and echoes. CharAncho is consumed with atavistic fear, when she feels the most delicate touch on her face she shrieks in terror.

"All is well," the voice says. "Soon you will know peace."

Something heavy steps carefully onto her legs.

She feels a sharp prick in her side, the flow of something cold. A pleasant numbness spreads through her. The voice is right, here is peace.

An odd wet mouth fumbles over her body. It pulses and presses, then extrudes some sticky mucilaginous thing half the length of her arm. It lies on her belly, palely luminous.

It is an egg.

All fear has gone, but CharAncho calmly reasons that this cannot be right. Surely her life should not end like this. She begins a desultory struggle. The creature holding her presses down and she struggles harder.

"My, you are a feisty one. Shall I sting you again?"

CharAncho forces herself to relax. A wave of dizziness washes over her, she fights her way back to consciousness and mumbles, "No need. I accept, I feel peace."

"Of course you do."

The weight holding her body eases. CharAncho feels detached from her body, a thing she still controls but barely inhabits. With one supreme effort she twists onto her stomach.

"Tricksy," the sibilant voice hisses. The weight comes again, but CharAncho rolls and carries it with her as she scrabbles across the dark, reaching, searching.

Her fingers touch the godsteel and fold around the hilt. In the same moment the creature flips her over onto her back and stings her again. Blind in the dark, CharAncho moves her arm across and back with her remaining strength. She feels resistance, she hears a horrifyingly loud high-pitched shriek.

CharAncho cannot feel her limbs. Does she still hold the blade? All sensations fade. Swaddled in layer upon layer of grey fog her mind falls away into a deeper void.

Peace.

#

Awestruck, Griem qa Jago sits like a statue, his eyes fixed on the godsteel. Beside him another of his band, Raghilt, whispers, "So it is true."

Griem gather himself. "We have followed the fire line questing for Rasteliger for two hundred cycles. We had hope but no... certainty. We followed a rumour, a legend, a dream. Now we see their work in your hands we know they are real."

"I'm sorry, this is not from Rasteliger's forge." AnphraJon says. "It is godsteel from an ancestor city, reforged from a rare weapon fetched down with one of the fallen."

Griem's band confer briefly, then he says, "It is still good news. Whatever lies above us, Rasteliger is from that place. It was they who built the road, and the bridge. If they still live they have the knowledge to make more godsteel."

A cautious exchange of existential beliefs begins. They soon reach the point where offence might be taken. Both groups agree that this will not happen because there will be no judgement on either side.

"What you call gods we think of as great creatures," Griem says. "But we believe there is a greater god, one that everyone and everything is sustained upon."

Once again LucusAna feels cut loose from his own beliefs. The ideas and philosophies Griem and his companions bring from their own city are not only strange they are also a complete and separate third way, neither Myxini or Aganathan.

"It was bad enough when there were two alternative truths," AnphraJon says later. "All three philosophies can't be right. Also, I don't much like the idea of walking on a god."

"Why not? You lived inside one all your life."

"Hmph."

Raghilt overhears and walks with them. "Griem is a fine leader, a good person. That said, not all of us cleave to the beliefs of the old city as strongly he does."

"Where was that, exactly?" LucusAna says.

"An outlier, far from the road." Raghilt makes an open-handed gesture. "It was a long time ago."

"Do you think Rasteliger is a god?"

Raghilt walks a few paces. "I don't know. When we find them we shall discover."

An unspoken question lies between the two groups—should they join forces? Griem's wanderers come out with the suggestion first.

LucusAna confers with his companions. AnphraJon is enthusiastic, RingenZaem less so. Like ThunusMunid, LucusAna thinks it is a pragmatic, sensible idea. There is strength in numbers, they are all heading in the same direction, the wanderers have far more experience of life on the surface.

ThunusMunid asks the obvious question. "Who will lead?"

"I lead family Jago," Griem says. "Raghilt leads Barabal. We aspire to nothing more."

LucusAna expects RingenZaem to propose herself as group leader, and he would support her. Instead, much to his surprise, she says, "LucusAna speaks for us." AnphraJon cheerfully agrees and ThunusMunid gives a wordless nod.

#

CharAncho lies without feeling, without sensation, her eyes wide open in the formless dark.

A dim light appears to be coming from one side of her own body, an eerie, gently pulsing gold-green glow. The strangeness of it, the sheer oddity, pulls her mind towards coherence. Her limbs feel connected to her like pieces of equipment, but she realises she can make them operate. It requires great concentration and several attempts but CharAncho eventually manages to heaver herself over onto her belly. Exhausted by the effort, she rests a while, then lurches upright. The queer green light rises with her.

She remembers the egg.

There it is, attached to her at her waist joint, between side and lower plates. Inside is sudden, flexing movement. A head, nothing but black eyes and saw-edged mouth-parts, stares out through the wall. Behind it, pale and legless, squirms a segmented body covered in clusters of small spines. The head turns and gnaws purposefully at the egg wall where it is attached to her body.

Panic wells up. She must get it off! Nothing has ever been more urgent. This *thing*, this carnivorous maggot will eat her alive from the inside out.

Her first hands grasp the egg. Where they touch, they stick. CharAncho pulls mightily but cannot detach the egg from her body or her hands from the egg. She pulls again, a broken sob bursts from her mouth. She is going to die here in the dark, horribly, awfully, slowly.

No, no, no.

The feel of godsteel in her second hand is utterly reassuring. For a moment she tries to prise the egg away from her body, then, with an incoherent exclamation at her own panicked stupidity, she slices through the egg case and through the creature inside.

It dies without complaint, with barely a reaction, so new to life it barely notices its own departure. Luminous gold-green liquid spills from the egg case, flares brightly for a few moments, then fades. The pulse of light lasts long enough for CharAncho to see what she most needs. It is a matter of moments to stagger across the dark chamber, take hold of the pull-bar and heave with all her strength.

Overhead the surface of the god road swings down and blessed light floods in. Now, for the first time, she can clearly see the horrors around her.

#

The god road winds towards the fire line between the branching pillars of black-smoke towers, and the wind steadily increases in strength. The tallest pillars are ten times LucusAna's height and he sees they seem to have built themselves up in pulses of flowing mudstone, oozing up from within. Every tower is smothered in a sliding, clambering mass of pale green-white crabs with tresses of long white hairs covering their claws. The largest is about the span of his hand, the smallest mere specks of life.

Here and there on the ground between the towers are solitary, black-shelled squat lobster, massively armoured, as long as LucusAna's arm, indolent and gorged, digesting their latest meal of hairy crab.

"I've never seen so much live food," LucusAna marvels.

"The thing is, those crabs taste disgusting," Raghilt says. "The lobster's good, but their shells are harder than bone and those claws can take off your finger."

Now they can feel the heat of the fire-line, a warmth on their bodies that promises to become unpleasantly strong. Even if there is a way across it is clear they will never be able to use it. The heat will kill them first.

Griem, Raghilt and the other wanderers spread out among the smoke towers to search for Rasteliger.

LucusAna suggests they help. RingenZaem wonders how. "I don't think they know what they are looking for."

"So they might not recognize it?"

"Quite."

"In which case they might have walked straight past this Rasteliger cycles ago," LucusAna says, thinking this is both funny and sad.

"But if Rasteliger did build the road, there's a good chance they are nearby," AnphraJon says.

The plumes of black smoke boiling up from the towers are pulled over by the wind and stream towards the fire line. Below them Griem and the others have stopped moving.

"A cylindrical head twenty times my height," AnphraJon declares. "Four simple eyes, one on top. A huge octago-nal-body, four arms like us, but with multiple joints and proportionately much longer."

It is such a specific description LucusAna stares at him.

"There's considerable damage." AnphraJon hurriedly scrawls in his notebook then mutely points. Now LucusAna sees what AnphraJon has seen and realises that in his mind, without knowing anything about Rasteliger at all, he has imagined a being much of their own size. The reality is that Rasteliger is big enough to be part of the landscape.

#

AmkaTan looks grimly down at the severed head CharAncho has just dropped at MakuraMazara's feet. Its features are both disturbingly like their own and unpleasantly different. It is not an easy sight.

"This is one of the things that has been taking our people," CharAncho declares.

Several priests-militant gather round. One of them prods the head with a godbone spear. "And now it's dead."

"One of," CharAncho repeats wearily. She tries to explain about the trap in the road; the glowing egg; that the monster could talk.

"Interesting if you're a scout," the priest says. "It's still dead."

"You're not listening," CharAncho says. The priest raises his first hands in mock horror and his companions laugh. CharAncho, hungry, tired, and hurting, has little time for such posturing. Somehow AmkaTan's hand, resting lightly but firmly on her shoulder, holds her back.

MakuraMazara's gaze sweeps over CharAncho. "How did you identify the trap?"

"I didn't. I saw nothing, no sign. The thing took me unawares."

DAVID GULLEN

The priests-militant smirk and shake their heads. Some scout.

CharAncho is genuinely angry now. "I didn't see you out there. What I heard is that you let people walk through your guard and now they are all dead."

The priests grip their god-bone spears. "We did our duty, three-arms."

CharAncho laughs. "You did nothing."

This is more than the priests can tolerate and change to a two-handed spear grip. CharAncho touches the hilt of her godsteel blade with a single finger. The priests look to her hand, a foolish move, for a warrior ever watches their opponent's eyes. All movements cease, nobody so much as breathes. CharAncho feels AmkaTan's presence behind her and wonders exactly where, if push came to shove, they would stand.

MakuraMazara, vice-philosopher and leader of the last of the Aganathans, shows her quality and walks between the two sides in a moment when movement from any quarter could trigger bloody mayhem.

"From now on we know we cannot rest or walk alone on the god road." MakuraMazara looks steadily towards the priests-militant then CharAncho. "And that is all."

AmkaTan stands at CharAncho's shoulder as the vice-philosopher and priests-militant walk away. "You've made enemies there."

He is right. CharAncho tries to remember the moment when she fell outside of MakuraMazara's regard. She knows she herself no longer really cares what the vice-philosopher thinks and wonders if that was that all it takes. To her surprise AmkaTan presses their brow against her own. "If I'm honest, you look terrible."

CharAncho looks at AmkaTan with new eyes. "I— I'm all right. Thank you. I could use something to eat."

"Easily remedied. Then, when you are rested and ready, I'd like to look at that trap, if you can find it again."

CharAncho has left the road trap open and even if it had somehow closed the paving there is soaked in blood from when she tossed up the severed head. "Ready when you are."

#

Now they are here, now they all stand in the shadow of that monumental, half-shattered entity called Rasteliger, LucusAna struggles to maintain his sense of self-worth. Falling into a brown study, he takes himself off to sit on a rock and attempt to think things through.

Only AnphraJon notices. He approaches with diffidence and sits in silence nearby. LucusAna sighs deeply then makes a fist and gently punches AnphraJon on his first shoulder. Thank you.

AnphraJon looks to where RingenZaem, Griem qa Jago and the others converse with Rasteliger. "It's not easy having a good time."

LucusAna gives a short, hard bark of laughter. As far as he can recall this is the first time AnphraJon has made a joke.

"What are we doing here, Jon?"

"You mean in terms of 'Why are we here at all?' and 'Why do we exist?'?"

"Something like that."

"You expect me to know! I'm flattered. Hang on, let me check my notes." AnphraJon opens his satchel, extracts one of his books and studiously scans the pages. "No... no... and no." He snaps the covers closed. "Nothing, sorry."

"All right, I take your point."

"Well, here's another. Why here, why now?"

LucusAna is silent. His hands tentatively form the Aganathan weave then fall apart. "Everything was so certain in the city, living in and on the godflesh. Even the dispute—the war—between us and the Myxini was understandable, I knew its origins and followed the reasoning, even if it was a form of mass stupidity. Everything that ever was, was there in the city. Except now I see it wasn't, because the city was a such small thing. As soon as I stuck my head out of that tunnel under the temple everything changed. Out here nothing feels...sure." LucusAna clutches the air with his all four hands. "Where's the certainty?"

AnphraJon wants to say, *Nothing changed except you. You grew up, is all. You opened your eyes and saw what anyone can see if they only they would bother to look.* But he is a full moult younger than LucusAna, two now, and although they have always been friends there is that gap and he is not sure how good, how deep and close, that friendship actually is. So he says nothing.

Unobserved, Raghilt qa Barabal has been listening. Where is certainty indeed. Feeling she has some good experience in that domain she joins the now silent pair.

"It seems to me that life, the world, the entirety of existence, has no essential inherent point. There is no secret direction, no observable destination."

"Perhaps these things are too big to see." AnphraJon has always enjoyed such debates.

"Perhaps they don't exist."

LucusAna emerges from within himself. "You say that as if it's a good thing."

"I believe so," Raghilt says. "Like you, I once worried, deeply and profoundly. Why am I here, where is my direction? I lived in a void. Then I realised I was free to decide what was important, not to the world, but to me. We are free create our own destiny."

"This is a useful way to look at things," AnphraJon says.

LucusAna thinks most people do not like having to think for themselves, and prefer universal certainties such as Aganathan philosophy or Myxini creed. *I have been that person,* he realises. *Yes, I am free to decide, but somehow I still believe. Not in the leaders or the priests, but in the teaching, the weave, that the One is All. Despite everything, my faith endures.* Could this be where certainty lies? The idea is comforting. "What does Rasteliger think?"

"We've only been talking about practical things," Raghilt says. "But we could go and ask them together."

The sheer fact of Rasteliger is beyond imagination, beyond LucusAna's ability to imagine. It is the source of his despondency, a lack in himself rather than the world. Although he doesn't much like this insight, he finds it easier to accept than a fault in the universe. "Let's do that," he says. Faith should be tested.

#

AmkaTan tells the other scouts where he and CharAncho are going and when they expect to return. While he does this, CharAncho fetches two livelight lanterns and feeds them a few scraps of godflesh. The livelights swoop onto the fragments and shred them with their ring-teeth. Watching them makes her hungry, and she eats again.

CharAncho leads the way down the god road. The walk does her good, the movement eases her physical aches and pains, the distance diminishes the antagonism she still feels towards the priests-militant. As they go she tells Amka-Tan everything she remembers: the creature's facility with speech, its paralysing sting, the horrible sight of the glowing egg stuck to her body. Towards the end of her tale she begins to shake with the memory of it. Strength leaves her legs and she needs to stop.

"Not everyone would have had the wherewithal to survive what you endured," AmkaTan says. "This... This reaction of your body is nothing to be ashamed of. One way or another everyone feels it after life has been in jeopardy." His voice quietens. "Me myself, more than once."

CharAncho says nothing. AmkaTan hazards a guess. "You are worried about going back. Wondering if you have enough courage."

It is the truth, CharAncho has never felt like this before. In the past, when every fight had been Myxini against Aganathan, warrior on warrior, she had felt nothing but joy—in the anticipation, in the moment, in the aftermath. Numbers were irrelevant, she stood alone, or with her brothers and sisters, those same priests-militant who now turned their backs on her. Whatever the odds she had only ever laughed.

She is far more afraid of how she will react than of the monster itself. This one *creature,* this person-thing, had bested her and her godsteel with nothing but the talents of its own body. Yes, she fears to meet another, fears to hear a quiet voice.

Rejoice....

CharAncho mutely nods.

"This time you're not alone," AmkaTan says.

When they arrive at the pit in the road they look down in silence. Sensing rot from the corpse below the livelights grow agitated and they hood the lanterns to stop the glow attracting wild swarms.

AmkaTan takes one of the lanterns, swings over the edge, hangs, and drops down. Livelight glow pushes shadow into the corners of the pit, a smaller place than CharAncho imagined in the dark.

Down there is the egg she sliced in two, hollow and drained. Down there is the headless corpse of the mother-thing with arms and legs folded close against its body in death. CharAncho climbs over the edge, less easily with her missing arm, and drops down beside him.

"This place is well-made," AmkaTan says. The stone walls have been dressed, the levers and rods supporting the hinged roof rotate in smooth sockets.

CharAncho inspects the mechanism and sees how the long poles have been made from belly and shoulder plates, skilfully split and glued with some dark resin. Revolted, she takes her hands away. "Us. These things are made from us."

AmkaTan's gaze comes to rest on the decapitated corpse of the creature that once lived here. "It is not the work of some animal."

It is something far worse.

"Over here." In the deep darkness of one of the corners CharAncho has discovered a recessed lever.

AmkaTan is ready. CharAncho pushes up. Silently, smoothly, the corners of the wall and floor fold away. A shallow ramp leads down into a darkness so thick it has texture.

CharAncho unhoods her lantern. Blue-white livelight illuminates the near end of a tunnel that descends in shallow steps, each tread as long as their own bodies.

Stepping silently, they descend.

#

Although LucusAna hears Rasteliger's voice, mild and toneless, free from all inflections, he sees no mouth. He turns his head and the speech moves with him. He listens intently and realises there is no voice, only words. The thoughts of the corroded legless giant appear directly in his mind.

Everyone has existential questions, but when Rasteliger hears of their encounter with the lampmouth it is immediately concerned with more practical things.

"Some of you will be infested with parasites. Come closer."

LucusAna is hesitant to move under the shadow of Rastliger's tilted bulk, but everyone else, from Griem qa Jago to AnphraJon immediately moves forward. Reluctantly, he follows, and steps into a vibration-aura as Rasteliger begins to hum, a sound so low he feels it more than hears, an all-pervasive and deeply unsettling sensation. LucusAna's fingertips tingle, his vision blurs, his innards quiver. All around his feet grit jumps and dances.

And his godsteel sings, the pure sound of sharp-edged metal being endlessly drawn across sharp metal.

AnphraJon shakes his head, slaps his brow with both hands and suddenly his whole body jerks. He flings something away with a shout of disgust.

LucusAna feels a growing discomfort along the soft underlap of his side plates, a spreading tickle, a sudden, rushing itch. Bubbles of clear liquid froth in the joints, then a segmented black worm erupts wriggling from the fluid and drops to the ground. In horrified revulsion he yells and stamps it to pulpy red smears. Something crawls in the corner of his vision, another worm. A second follows, he feels it wriggling behind his eye. In a frenzy of disgust and fright he knocks them off his face and stamps on them, stamps on them again.

Twenty of the parasites are driven from his body. For AnphraJon and three of Griem's group, including Raghilt, it is the same.

The vibrations fade, LucusAna hears Rasteliger's voice. "You are free of them."

"Thank you." LucusAna still feels sick, the thought of those things living inside him disgusting. Words are not enough to fully express his gratitude. For the first time he sees Rasteliger for what it is—a thinking being, though not made of flesh. A crippled titan, but still alert, still wise. And possessed of a spontaneous kindness he would never have suspected in one so broken and strange and vast.

Griem puts LucusAna's thoughts into words: "We sought you out to ask for help. Instead, you helped us. How can we repay you?"

Rasteliger's words come into their minds. "Before we come to that, tell me why you came."

"Two things," Griem says, "Weapons better than godbone, and a way across the fire line."

"And you?" Rasteliger directs his words at LucusAna's group.

"Knowledge," AnphraJon replies.

"Adventure," says RingenZaem.

For LucusAna there can only be one question. Yet he fears to speak, uncertain if he really wants to know the answer. But he has seen too much and the need to know burns within him like his own internal fire-line. In his heart he is convinced the Myxini are wrong and the Great Solitary is a myth. God flesh is just that, the flesh of gods, their meat and bone. "Why do the gods fight?"

For a long moment Rasteliger is silent, then:

"Knowledge? Ask.

"Weapons? I shall make them.

"Adventure is not within my gift, it is yours to choose."

RingenZaem laughs and bows her head.

DAVID GULLEN

"A way across the fire-line exists. As for the gods and what they do… I can only tell my story." Rasteliger's breathless sigh carries a welter of emotions. Grief, loneliness, and dull anger are merely the first layer. "LucusAna, I know you carry godsteel for I heard it sing. Give it to me. This is my price, it is the only thing you have that I want."

AnphraJon gasps. There is nothing more valuable than godsteel in the whole wide world.

"You do not have to do this, Ana," RingenZaem says.

LucusAna feels Griem and Raghilt's eyes on him and understands they will accept his decision.

But he will, and he wants to. The third part of his life begins here and, perhaps, enlightenment. It feels right that it begins with a gift and sacrifice, a casting off. He unsheathes the godsteel blade and offers it to Rasteliger on the palms of his first hands.

Rasteliger reaches down with an arms ten times longer than LucusAna's own body. A finger extends into a multi-jointed limb carrying a smaller hand. A finger of this hand unfolds a slender arm ending in a third hand the size of a child's. This hand takes the blade and withdraws.

"Now we can begin," Rasteliger says.

#

The tunnel descends to a dark gallery that runs both left and right. The air is cool, sharp with smell of damp stone and, faintly, something else, something sour and sharp and meaty. Instinctively they hood their lanterns so only the thinnest sliver of light shows.

"Left, or right?" CharAncho whispers. There is nothing to help them choose.

As they hesitate AmkaTan sees a minuscule glimmer away in the left-side distance. She closes her lantern completely and motions for CharAncho to do the same. Utter darkness envelopes them.

The light draws nearer, swaying and jouncing. Still dim and distant it develops a gold-green glow. CharAncho recognises it for what it is, egg-light. "One of them comes."

She feels AmkaTan's hand on her arm as he urges her back into the tunnel. AmkaTan's voice comes close against her face, soft as breath. "When I say 'Now', attack. Until then, do nothing."

"I will," CharAncho murmurs, though her hand shakes. She finds the hilt of her godsteel and grips it.

The gold-green glow is closer now. It pulses and ebbs in a way the first egg never did. Along with it comes an indistinct murmur of speech. All at once the light divides and with crippling fear CharAncho knows there are two eggs, carried by two Mothers. These things live in the dark, their tails sting, and they are quick, startlingly, horrifyingly quick. She doubts herself, she doubts her own courage. For the first time in her life she doubts she can win a fight.

Motionless beside her, AmkaTan says nothing.

CharAncho knows if she runs they will catch her. First, they will catch AmkaTan and fix an egg to him. Then they will catch her and she too will die. Despite knowing this, atavistic horror claws inside. Before the fight there is the fight against an unfamiliar and powerful enemy—herself.

How she wants to run.

CharAncho takes one slow and silent step back through the darkness, then another.

The two Mothers draw near, their words coming clear. Sharp claws click on stone. With them comes the first waft of something both repellent and enticing—old meat and sweetness.

"...I just think we're incredibly lucky. This swarming or migration of the nurses happens, what, once every twenty generations? And here we are, you and me. We'll have a nurse for every single one of our little cuties, everyone will."

"We need to understand why these swarms happen, try more captive breeding."

"We don't even know what they eat. Well, we do, but where does that revolting flab come from? Good times, bad times, whatever the cause it's our good time now and my little girl is going to eat all she wants and grow big and strong."

"Aw, look at her all cosy and snug in her egg."

"Yours too, what a delight." The Mothers laugh and it is the coldest, unkindest sound CharAncho had ever heard. "Soon we'll have the numbers. We should take out Hive Nine and the migration route will be ours."

They are very close now.

"We need Hive Nine for their drones."

"True, sadly true, though their heads are so tasty."

"You are dreadful."

"You know it makes them pump harder- Oh, can you smell that nurse stink?"

The susurrus scrape of their feet halts.

"Joi laid early and went ahead, remember?"

"Oh, yes, it's probably her. Which is her tunnel?"

"It's just ahead."

The two Mothers resume walking. Their easy confidence, the naturalness of their hideous conversation makes CharAncho's body crawl like moult-itch. She cannot move.

They are here.

Egg-light reflects off the tunnel corner. The stone glitters, it's beautiful, really. CharAncho sees AmkaTan quietly draw his godbone blade. He holds the hooded livelight lamp in one secondary hand and unscrews the lid with the other. He does not look back.

"Now." AmkaTan throws the lidless lamp and rushes around the corner. Livelights burst free, blue-white light floods the tunnel.

CharAncho does not move.

"It's alive!" one of the Mothers yelps.

Shadows blur and swing under the swirling livelight glow.

"Ooh, mine!"

"Careful, it has a thing, a stick!"

"My sting will calm it."

CharAncho watches monstrous shadow-limbs, heads and bodies leap in outsized motion across the walls. She hears the skitter of claws, heavy bellows-breath, the dull slap of godbone against dense body plates. Paralysed with fear, she can go neither forward nor back.

High and hoarse, AmkaTan calls her name.

#

"We were made, not born, my brothers and I," Rasteliger tells them. "Given bodies and minds, then sent down to build the road, bridge the fire-line, and gather the harvest."

"By the gods." LucusAna is in awe.

"Gods? Perhaps. They are not of this world, but neither am I." Rasteliger gestures at their own ruination, "And I am no god."

"For a brief while I lived under the bright sky of that dazzling place of creation and invention. Life was lived at a pace I find astonishing to remember. Knowing no different, I took it for granted. Now, perhaps because it was so long ago, I wonder if it real or a kind of dream? Then I remember I was made, not born. I cannot dream, so it was real.

"Our creators ordered us down to your world and we descended, happy to do the work for which we had been made. For the work was us and we were the work.

"When all our tasks were complete they called with irresistible words and for a second time I saw the bright world. But they were finished with us, for the work was done and so were we. One by one we went uncomplaining to the machine of unmaking. I was the last but before my turn came the machine broke, unmade by its own unnmaking. What was left of me was dragged aside and flung back down. Down and down I fell, and landed here."

AnphraJon asks a question, then another. Griem and Raghilt join in, RingenZaem too. Standing among them LucusAna's mind reels. There is a sky above this sky? A higher world exists yet the gods are not there either. Do they inhabit a third world? And if there is a third world could there be a fourth? *We are the work,* Rasteliger said, *The work was us.* All he can think of is the Aganathan mantra: *All is One; The One is All.* How can he make sense of such a simple, dependable message in a world grown so intricate and large? He decides that if the gods are not actually gods, then the real gods must surely work through them. This, surely, must be true. Worlds above worlds, therefore gods above gods.

He struggles to make sense of this, to accept it. Unbidden, an idea comes into his mind—what if the tiers of worlds have no end and therefore the true gods are impossibly, unimaginably remote? No, he tells himself over and again. Thoughts are not facts, this simply cannot be. He must have faith.

He knows AnphraJon would say he is begging the question, unwilling to accept the truth that sometimes truth is unknown. Needs be, he must believe. What else is there?

Rasteliger looks up at the empty dark sky. "I cannot dream, but I can hope. And my hope is that I shall mend myself, that one day I might rise and return to the bright world. Your gift of godsteel is the first step on that path. It contains rare elements I need for repairs. Then, I will be able to move and find more of what I need. And then I will-"

AnphraJon is filled with concern. "Won't they just-? Won't they break you again? The gods."

"They have taken what they wanted from your world," Rasteliger replies. "They are long gone."

#

CharAncho draws her blade and throws herself round the corner on shaking knees. She feels she moves in slow-motion, clumsy, ponderous, useless.

AmkaTan faces off against the two Mothers. They have their tails up, the stingers beaded with venom. They jostle each other and laugh as they vie for first strike.

"Another one!"

"Convenient. Mine?"

"Yours."

AmkaTan side-steps, darts in, jumps back, dodges one stinger strike and blocks the other. Venom drops spatter, livelights swoop and pulse overhead.

"Stand still, feisty one. My baby needs her nursey-nurse."

The Mothers move as one, astonishingly quick. One springs directly at AmkaTan, the other at CharAncho in a two-step leap that bounces her high off the tunnel wall.

CharAncho reacts instinctively, the muscle memory of a hundred fights. Godsteel meets armoured chitin, her two-handed cut lops an arm, severs a foot. The Mother creature crashes down awkwardly, her sting buried in CharAncho's shoulder.

"You will regret that, I promise," the creature hisses.

Numbness spreads from CharAncho's shoulder, already her head swims. She has been here before and knows she has only moments. She throws herself forwards, godsteel outthrust. Her crippled foe lurches awkwardly. CharAncho topples onto her, her weight drives the tip of her blade into the Mother's eye, her head, her brain, and so she dies.

"Amka... godsteel." CharAncho's words slur, she tries to pull the weapon free but she is fading, her mind disconnected from body. Once again movement is theory, desire merely opinion. She is nowhere.

The surviving Mother is aghast. "What have you done? What of the egg? This outcome is neither correct nor desired."

"I disagree." Reaching back, AmkaTan knocks CharAncho's limp hand from the godsteel hilt and pulls the blade free. He snaps it down and up, flicking gore and brains onto the floor and roof.

Now it is his time to laugh.

#

For the second time following a Mother's sting CharAncho's mind lurches into awareness. This time she quickly becomes fully alert, her body obeys her mind's desires and she regains her feet. AmkaTan returns her sword.

"Thank you."

"I should thank you. For a moment there..." AmkaTan opens his mouth, closes it, and opens it again. "It doesn't matter."

Side by side they look down on the corpses of the two Mothers. CharAncho takes her godsteel and slices through one of the glowing eggs, killing the larva inside. Gold-green luminescent ichor spurts across the belly plates of the corpse. Slowly the glow dissipates. AmkaTan destroys the second egg and the scrap of life inside quietly expires.

CharAncho swallows, looks down, and braces herself for what she knows she must say, "I was scared," she confesses. "You were right to doubt me."

AmkaTan methodically cleans his own blade, wiping its edge on the shoulder of the Mother he killed, first one side then the other. "In the end you did not desert me." He looks straight at CharAncho, "I say there is nothing to be ashamed of here. We both fought, we both killed, and we both live."

A gust of relief blows through CharAncho. She is forgiven, her faults and failings forgiven, and she realises it is this fractured, fragile trust that binds ordinary warriors together. Courage has its limits and no-one is infallible. In this moment she would do anything for AmkaTan. "What now?"

AmkaTan looks past the ruin of the two corpses towards the dark tunnel and says, in a tone that implies his suggestion is of little consequence, "I quite fancy taking a look down there."

This is a test CharAncho will not fail. She replies in the same light manner. "That sounds insanely dangerous."

AmkaTan laughs silently. "Definitely."

"So what are we waiting for?"

CharAncho still has her hooded lantern and opens it the bare minimum. They step over the bodies and walk into darkness. Behind them, the freed livelights from the other lantern drift down onto the corpses. Each dabs at the ichor and other fluids with tip of their proboscis, then settles first to drink, then mate, and lay their own eggs.

#

The unlit tunnel gradually curves away to the right. Pacing carefully and quietly CharAncho becomes aware of a low murmuring that shifts and surges like the echoes of wind-blown sand. She taps AmkaTan on the shoulder and touches her own ear. AmkaTan nods, he hears it too.

Ahead, a glimmering of reflected light shines on the left wall, pale and even. The tunnel's curve unwinds into a straight section and they see that a long run of the right-hand wall is open from roof to floor, excepting a dozen rough columns. Through the gaps come light and sound, a murmuring babble of distant voices. They both stop, eyes wide and ears open.

CharAncho slides the shutter on her lantern closed.

They pad stealthily forwards, one leg at a time.

They reach the edge of the first gap and look through.

They see a tiered vista of rocky levels, platforms and winding ramps under the roof of a broad and lofty cavern. Connecting walkways hang between the levels at various heights. Clusters of woven white fibrous domes cling to the walls and the levels, some even hang beneath the walk-ways. There are hundreds of them. Everywhere, in ceaseless motion, emerging and disappearing into the domes, walking on the levels, ramps, and walkways, are a host of Mothers, each carrying an egg glowing with gold-green light.

AmkaTan's hand fumbles for her arm, grips, and pulls. CharAncho follows AmkaTan's gaze downwards. The entire floor of the cavern is covered in heaps and drifts of desic-cated corpses, layer upon numberless layer. Heads and arms, legs, stinger tails, disconnected plates and whole bodies lie piled beneath the levels, scree slopes of the dead a hundred feet high. It is impossible to tell how deep they go.

They look on in silence, as still as the cold stone that surrounds them. All across the city Mothers scurry and swarm the walls around their white nests. The sounds of their multitude voices, the click and scratch of their clawed feet fill the air with a soft cacophony.

A paralysing dread seeps into CharAncho as she remembers the words of one of the Mothers they killed. "Soon we'll have our own swarm", it had said, then, "We need Hive Nine for their drones."

This is not their only city.

"Come away." CharAncho tugs on AmkaTan's arm, but it is as if he has turned to stone. "We have to go. Now."

AmkaTan shudders and turns CharAncho a look of wall-eyed fear she well understands. She takes his first hands in her own and leads him away.

#

Once they have climbed out of the tunnels and up onto the god road CharAncho does nothing but stand and breathe. She looks across the rolling grey landscape, up at the empty sky, down at her own feet on the stonework of the road. Although she has not slept, she feels she has woken from a horrible dream.

They both start walking at the exact same moment, towards where vice-philosopher MakuraMazara waits for them with the main body of Aganathan refugees. Soon after, again at the exact same moment, they step off the road and continue along its side.

After a while AmkaTan says, "How's your shoulder?"

"It's all right."

They know it shouldn't take this long to get back but neither of them wants to admit it, or stop, or sleep. Neither of them wants to risk dreams, not yet. Finally, near the point of exhaustion, they halt. It has been obvious for a long time that MakuraMazara has not bothered to wait for them. The main body of the Aganathans is long gone.

They rest for a while. Then, with nothing else to do, walk on.

AmkaTan points across the barren landscape. "Over there."

CharAncho sees the blue-white glow of a livelight lamp. It cuts towards them and AmkaTan hurries forward with renewed energy to greet one of his scouts.

#

Unable to dissuade MakuraMazara from marching on, the scouts describe how they watched her lead the refugees away.

"They would not listen to us and stayed on the road," one of the scouts said without heat. "Every cycle they lost another twenty to those creatures."

AmkaTan tells the scouts their own story. They have questions on detail but accept her tale without doubt.

"Perhaps we should warn them again," CharAncho wonders.

"You can only say the same thing so many times," the scout replies.

AmkaTan agrees. "There's nothing we can do. You'd need an army and we—" His gesture encompasses the small group. "We are not an army."

It is obvious to CharAncho the scouts are better off out here on their own. Scouts do not need cities, they do not need roads, they certainly do not need MakuraMazara. Unlike her, they know the grey land and can live here indefinitely. There are enough of them to start again, to found a new way of living.

It is possible, she thinks, that enough of the Aganathans will reach the new city before they are extinguished. She has her doubts.

She realises everyone else is sitting quietly, not looking anywhere in particular.

"I am not a scout," she ventures, trying to find a way through her own thoughts.

"Yet you could be," AmkaTan says.

"Ay-ha," say the gathered scouts. This is true.

"Neither am I Aganathan."

"There are no Aganathan's here," AmkaTan says. "Not really."

"I know..." More than anything CharAncho does not want to offend. "I know I would be welcome."

"But." AmkaTan says.

"But not yet." She speaks slowly as realisation comes. "There is one more thing I must do."

They give her gifts: a second knife, her satchel filled with food, a small cannister of livelight eggs. She has nothing, except one thing. It feels right.

"May I see your blade?" she asks AmkaTan.

It is a fine thing, a single piece of black godbone from hilt to tip, the edge neither blunt nor honed too fine.

"I would like to borrow this, and lend you mine."

AmkaTan receives CharAncho's godsteel blade with reverence. "This is a mighty gift."

"Ay-ha," the scouts say.

"You have given me more," CharAncho says.

AmkaTan sheathes his new blade then offers his hand. CharAncho takes it, their fingers interlace in the Aganathan weave because some things do not change and some things still mean something.

"Come back," AmkaTan says. "If you can."

"Ay-ha," say the scouts.

#

Rasteliger keeps their word and provides them with weapons: long-handled spears and true swords, seamless, pale yellow, and smooth. RingenZaem and the experienced warriors in Griem's group handle the blades with reverence, impressed by their lightness, good balance, and unusual colour.

"Sharper than godsteel," Rasteliger tells them.

"Harder than black bone," Raghilt cuts, thrusts, and rolls her chosen blade. "Better by far." She and Griem talk excitedly about crossing the fire-line.

LucusAna realises there is nothing to keep them here. As soon as they are ready they will go. What brief fellowship the two groups once had, formed from mutual convenience, it is over.

"I've decided to go with them," RingenZaem says. "Who knows what sights we'll see, what we'll find?" She rubs her hands together. "Adventure." She looks to each one of her companions, the people she has been with since fleeing the city, and takes a breath. Everyone hears the hope in her voice. "Come with me?"

There is a moment of silence.

"Not me." ThunusMunid walks away.

"Part of me..." AnphraJon exhales slowly, one of his second hands covers his mouth. "I could... I would like to see, very much..." He shakes the thoughts away. "I will stay with Rasteliger. There is much for me to learn."

LucusAna and RingenZaem have always got along well, always there was the thought in the back of his mind that maybe, after final moult they might bond. He likes her, likes her a lot, but he also knows that is as far as it goes. Is that enough to leave everything behind forever? He knows the answer before he has finished framing the question.

It strikes him that perhaps this is not meant for him: pair-bonding, the peace of egg time, the joy of children. The gods, while they war, still make plans and he feels this onward journey is not for him. Two times what he thought of as more than friendship ended in disaster, betrayal and hurt. GalaTheo, his first true friend, tried to kill him. CharAncho, the one with whom he first shared moult-feast, the only one that ever made him feel like they were two arms of the same body, turned her back on him in his moment of need. Both chose faith and duty rather than loyalty in friendship. These are lessons, he decides, and also messages. He must learn from them.

"I—" LucusAna shakes his head. He need say no more. He is as certain he is right as he is that he is making a mistake.

RingenZaem jerks her shoulders and looks away. "All right."

#

Brooding, silent ThunusMunid leaves them within the cycle. She does not say farewell. LucusAna suspects her self-imposed quest to kill every lampmouth she can find will only end one way.

For the rest of them their final meal together is a gentle, happy one. Old stories are told, good ones that end well, that end in laughter.

It is a meal none of them will ever forget. Faces are remembered, and the laughter. So near to parting, they have never felt closer. One by one they fall asleep where they sit.

When LucusAna wakes everyone else has made their way to where Rasteliger sits, closer to the fire-line. He sees Griem qa Jago climb onto Rasteliger's hand, where it lies palm upwards on the ground. Rasteliger's fingers close to form a cage, flanges extend from the sides of each finger joint and the hand becomes a hollow ball. Swiftly Rasteliger's arm extends enormously, carrying Griem through the leaping flames of the fire-line. When it withdraws, the mid-section glows red with heat. Blurred through the fire and smoke, small with distance, Griem stands on the far side of the fire-line and waves.

One by one they are gone. Rasteliger's arm retracts and they subside back into their normal mountainous form.

"What happened to the bridge," AnphraJon asks.

"There was never a bridge," Rasteliger replies. "I am the bridge." Their vast tubular head sinks down and the lights in their eyes fade to glimmers. The constant wind pulled in by the fire-line rips black smoke from the nearest towers. Sheets of flame leap, ebb, roar, and leap again. There is nothing else.

Rasteliger becomes alert. AnphraJon's posture changes and LucusAna realises he and the ruined titan are talking. With nothing else to do, he wanders and finding himself close to the god road, walks towards it.

As he steps onto it, the ground trembles and an intense yellow light throws long, flat shadows. Rasteliger had completed the repairs he needed the godsteel for and the half-ruined mechanical titan rises on a ring of a hundred jets of yellow flame. Trailing tangled cables, twisted frame-works and broken cladding, Rasteliger drifts away down the fire-line with increasing speed. LucusAna sees AnphraJon standing on a fenced platform high on Rasteliger's shoulder. Melancholy vies with happiness as he watches them vanish into the far distance. Everyone follows the path that called them, all that remains is for him to find his own.

Alone but not lonely, LucusAna returns back along the god road the way he came.

#

The cycles pass as if in a dream. The mountains rise up, he passes through them, they fall behind. The fire-line is no more than a low band of red light.

Up in the formless dark a slow sliding movement tugs LucusAna's eye. Impossibly high, far out across the empty lands he now knows are not empty, a titanic grey silhouette is painted in the dark sky. It is blunt-headed, with long side-fins and a two-lobed horizontal tail. Three rows of flickering lights span its stupendous length. For long moments his mind refuses to accept the impossible scale of it, a colossus that hangs unsupported amidst nothing. Compared to this, Rasteliger is a grain of sand.

With its head lower than the tail, the great shape slowly descends, vast and serene. As he stands and gapes, a swarm of glimmering motes erupt from the belly, each formed from an inverted cup above a dependent stem. The mote-swarm rises swiftly and is soon lost to view.

What is he looking at? Is it still alive, was it once alive, is it a made thing? Whatever it is, one thing is clear. LucusAna starts to laugh, a dry and bitter sound. By bringing him here, to this astonishing encounter, the gods have revealed something extraordinary—they do not exist. At least, not in any of the ways he has been taught to believe. If this is a descending godflesh city—and what else can it be—this once inhabited and now abandoned thing is neither a dying god nor a cast-off fragment. Everything the Myxini fought so hard to defend is false, Aganathan philosophy is false.

Insights overwhelm him. Nobody had ever known, the first had only guessed. Later, others hoped, and finally we decided to believe. His mind accepts this but in the moment his heart refuses. It is too much. He will pretend for a while, then deny it is pretence, then fall silent, accepting his eyes have grown a little clearer. In truth his journey has just begun.

Far along the god road LucusAna sees a figure as transfixed as he is by the sight of the descending colossus. A god but not a god, a god that is a falling vessel, a dying creature, an abandoned house. All of these things. None of them.

Raghilt's words come back to him—he must seek his own truths.

LucusAna feels one overriding imperative, to go to where this strange titan will descend. He can survive out here, with care and good fortune he will complete the journey, no matter how long it takes. The journey is not what daunts him, it is the arrival. He does not want to be there alone.

He sets out along the god road towards the lone figure, taking his time, letting his tumultuous thoughts settle into some semblance of order. As he draws nearer he realises he knows who it is, and he laughs a second time. They are still a good distance apart when CharAncho holds up her hand in greeting. After a moment he does the same, overwhelmingly glad to see her again, anticipating the moment when their hands clasp in the Aganathan weave.

It comes to him then that the weave is still a truth, symbolism not of faith but of life. That a life lived is interwoven with other lives, that it is threaded through with things beyond experience and control. Everything is interlaced.

He hurries forward, eager to tell CharAncho his sudden insight, thinking also about what has transpired between them since they left the city. He finds he can accept it all, that it lies far behind him in a distant, different heart.

This is a new time.

To Sail the Interstice

Ben Wright

TO SAIL THE INTERSTICE

The Rust Graveyard

Garnas reeled in his line, resigned to the fact that he would catch no more fish that day. It wasn't a bad haul for an afternoon's work but he'd hoped for more. The day had started bright but the weather had become wrong, at least for fish. A stiff offshore breeze carried wild scents from the jungle. Garnas looked over the canopy, where the clouds stirred. If they had been over the sea, he would have predicted a storm for sure, but the winds inland danced to stranger influences than temperature and pressure.

Seagulls bickered on the side of the cliff above him. If they had given up fishing for the day it was wise to follow their example. Time to head home. If there was a storm, better to avoid it.

The packed earth path was known to turn to mud in the rain, and it ran steeply up onto the headland to the south. Treacherous in the extreme in wet conditions but taxing exercise in any weather. Garnas was the only one who used it these days. He'd hammered metal spikes into the ground alongside it, something to hold on to if he ever got caught in a downpour. He always came here alone, and was acutely aware of the danger should he become injured. This was a land that devoured the careless.

The wind whipped his coat around him as he walked. He set down his bucket and rod to tie it more tightly. He'd salvaged the thick waterproof fabric himself. It was stronger and warmer than garments woven from grey hemp. It marked him as someone who had been into the jungle in search of spoils—and one of the few with the right mix of

94

bravery and caution to succeed. Something about this coast caught the imagination, instilled wild ideas of wandering into the unknown. Garnas had never succumbed to it. No-one would have blamed him if he had.

He'd reached the graveyard now. There was a low boundary wall, long consumed by brambles and uncultivated hemp. Orange rust stains were all that remained of its north gate. The graveyard itself was no less swamped by foliage. There was only one path through it, a narrow way cut through branches more than ten feet high. It fell to Garnas to keep it clear, now, with sickle and shears. The path ran in defiance of how the graveyard had originally been laid out. Signs remained of the original design: brick paths and the stumps of low iron fences. Most prominent were the iron grave markers themselves. The salt air had gone to work on them almost immediately they had been laid and now they were nothing but lumps of rust, flaking away day by day.

Garnas didn't know why its builders had chosen this spot. It was the highest point visible along the coast and thus caught the worst of the weather. The graveyard was just one of their inscrutable artefacts, and scarcely the largest. Garnas knew, intellectually, that they were probably his ancestors, but he felt no sense of kinship with them. The marks they had left on the land—great, dirty marks at that—seemed to hold no meaning. Even the action of the waves on the rocks seemed more relatable, more human somehow. The preoccupations of his forebears were truly alien and undeniably invasive.

Was there another Garnas buried there somewhere? An antecedent whose only legacy was a name passed down to the present day? He had often wondered but there was no way to know. Perhaps his parents would have known, but he had never thought to ask them until it was too late. He passed under the arch of the south gate without a backwards glance.

Without the walls to obscure his view, he could look down the slope of the headland to the town. The river mouth was a natural harbour, at least for ships with a shallow draught, and the town was perched right where it met the sea. It was far less impressive when you realised most of the buildings were derelict. You could tell which were still in use by the way the corrugated iron roofs were patched. Those open to the sky had already been completely cannibalised. One day there would be no more usable roofing material left. Perhaps then some would have to be salvaged from the jungle.

The eye was never drawn to the town, however. The river stole the show. A river of rust—harsh orange with the glint of an oily film on the surface. Laden with iron motes, it laboured through the channel and into the open sea. Its stain spread out in a great plume to be lost in the vastness of the ocean. Only eventually, though; the sea was discoloured for miles around. Sailors lost in fog could determine their distance from the town by the colour of the waters alone. Nothing lived in that tainted river, not even algae. It was the reason Garnas had to head so far up the coast to find fish.

The town itself was not responsible for the condition of the river. Its water was already spoiled by the time it left the jungle. The river banks were bare, too toxic even for the hardiest jungle flora. The sting of the river in his nostrils meant 'home' to Garnas.

The wind had picked up. At the edge of the town, Garnas waved to someone working amongst neat rows of canes with grey hemp growing up them.

"Any luck?" she called, then had to snatch a fish out of the air.

"Judge for yourself." He laughed, jokingly threatening to throw another.

She pulled a face, pretending to be annoyed, then ducked around the corner of the house to put the fish in the smoker.

"Persinian was looking for you," she said when she returned.

"What about?"

"Visitors." She nodded towards the harbour.

The town was such a familiar sight that Garnas seldom paid it any real attention. He looked up now and saw what he had missed earlier: a ship pulled in at the wharf. A barque, by the look of the masts, with its sails furled. The wharf—another relic of the bygone age—was almost comically too large for the ship. When he pictured it, Garnas still saw the looming crane hanging over it, but that landmark had finally collapsed five years ago. The remains of it still dragged in the river like a lazy arm. The ship had pulled up to the dock just short of it.

Garnas had been very excited at visitors when he was a youngster. They had always come from across the sea, of course; there was no other settlement anyone knew of on the coast, and it was doubtful there even could be one. It would have taken a monumental effort to steal even this little patch of land from the jungle, an effort that was ultimately proving futile. The idea that such effort would have been duplicated elsewhere was preposterous—although someone had gone looking for one once, just the same.

It wasn't the largest ship Garnas had seen and he was aware he hadn't seen many. Smaller ones were not uncommon visitors when he was a boy. Only two ships had put to shore over the last three years though. The ship had its sails on show, suggesting it was planning to leave before long. Garnas doubted they'd manage to beat the storm, if one was indeed coming. Still, they presumably knew their business better than he did.

Persinian, as the de facto headman of their settlement, generally dealt with any visitors. There was always tension between the townspeople and the sailors. There was a lack of trust in either direction, coupled with a reluctance to be the first side to visibly break faith. It was just easier if Persinian handled discussions alone. He claimed to have travelled on the sea once himself, but that was something Garnas couldn't picture him doing, even as a much younger man.

By the time Garnas reached the dock, the ship had rolled its sails up completely. This was also concerning; traders were given a limited welcome but Persinian insisted they never stayed overnight.

The old man was sitting on a rusted bench under the eaves of an old warehouse.

"Ah, Garnas," he wheezed.

"What's the problem?" Persinian's expression confirmed what Garnas suspected.

"These guests arrived soon after you left this morning," Persinian explained. "They brought some bits and pieces to trade. Good stuff; things we were running short of."

Garnas waited for him to get to the point. Trying to hurry him never worked.

"They also had a couple of passengers. Adventurous sorts. They wanted to explore a little and I could not dissuade them. The ship's captain made it clear she'd put them ashore elsewhere if I refused to let them disembark. Against my better judgement, I acquiesced. They were last seen heading into the jungle, promising to return by noon."

Garnas couldn't suppress a gasp.

"I know, so very foolish. They looked able to handle themselves and I thought they would know better than to venture too far."

Persinian shrugged, an admission of error.

"They have not returned."

The glances they exchanged said it all. The jungle was hazardous enough for those who knew it well, travelling in groups of four or five. If the visitors were overdue they should be assumed dead.

Persinian continued: "The captain says she won't leave until they return or she's sure they're dead. She says she's prepared to stay four more days, if necessary. I feel it is imprudent for us to try and force them to leave."

Garnas nodded.

"You want me to search for them?"

"Trelden and Margha are still fixing the paddock fences, but they should be back tonight. Tomorrow morning, take them and whoever else you need and mount a search. Find evidence that the visitors met their end and bring it back. Something that will satisfy the good captain."

Garnas looked up at the sky. It was still impossible to tell if a storm would come.

"I'll leave now. Have Margha lead a rescue party tomorrow if I'm not back before then."

Persinian looked pained.

"It's not urgent that they leave. The captain has a point. In the circumstances, one overnight stay is quite reasonable."

"It's not that," Garnas said, putting down his bucket of fish pointedly. "We don't know they're dead. They might be holed up somewhere. What if we find them tomorrow and discover they could have been rescued if someone reached them earlier? I won't have that on my conscience."

"Who can you take? Trelden, Margha and Nenji are across the river. Stervin's deep in his cups already, and Mattrel's poorly. No-one else has much experience in the jungle."

"I'll go alone." Garnas hardened his expression when Persinian started to object. "No-one knows it like me. I'll not take unnecessary risks. If I find them, I can keep them safe until morning. If not, I can keep *myself* safe until morning."

"Garnas—"

"It's my decision," Garnas's voice was harsh with determination, even though he tried to soften it out of respect for his elder.

"You don't have to do this," Persinian said gently. "I know why you want to. Your parents—"

The hiss of indrawn breath warned the old man he'd gone too far.

"I'll tell Margha," he finished, sadly. "May all the luck be with you."

#

The wind couldn't make itself felt at ground level, but it could be heard roaring through the upper levels of the canopy. It was weather where you had to be inside someone else's hood to make yourself heard. Almost enough to make Garnas glad he was alone and didn't need to make himself heard. Almost.

He kept close to the river, where the trees were sparser. He saw three large jungle cats moving slowly between the trunks a few hundred yards into the interior. He could see them, which meant they weren't hunting, but he paid them close attention anyway. The jungle did not have an apex predator, but it did have four or five species enthusiastically vying for that title. The cats were but one of them.

Following the river was a mistake. It might mean you could move more quickly, but you had your back against a figurative wall. Even if you could fight off dangerous fauna, the noise and the blood would bring more animals—or worse. Following the river was a mistake, but it was a mistake Garnas guessed the missing explorers had made.

His hunch was confirmed by scraps of cloth on a resin-bush. The plant was one of the few without vicious thorns, which made it look less dangerous to the naïve eye. Its leaves secreted a quick-setting adhesive that hardened to a bond with greater tensile strength than leather. If the wanderers had continued into that harmless-looking patch of bluish undergrowth, they would still be there now. As it was they had only left behind one blue sleeve. At least they hadn't tried burning the leaves away. Their resin was a natural accelerant.

Garnas found himself following a narrow strip of soft ground alongside the river. To his left an intimidating wall of thorns threaded its way up a steep incline. It looked to be an old bank of the river, one that had been undermined over time until the lip had collapsed into the strand he now found himself on. The soil sparkled in the overcast light, betraying metallic contamination. He checked the coal in his long gun and was happy to see it still smouldered. Although in such close confines it would not help much, should he be attacked.

The damp path yielded onto cracked and stained concrete. Untold decades of weathering had exposed steel reinforcing rods, which in turn had corroded to almost nothing. The river edge of the concrete was in fragments and held together only by those few rods remaining. Gantries that had once been suspended over the river lay immersed in it like languid arms from a lazy boat. Ahead of Garnas a massive structure towered, wreathed in vines. The holes of old windows had been forced wider by tree-trunks twisting through them; or perhaps the great trees, hundreds of feet tall, were wearing the remains of the building like stiff clothes.

Factory One.

The war might have been going the jungle's way, but it was not without losses. Substances more noxious than mere iron and concrete still lay in sumps, gutters and leaking barrels. More than half the trees Garnas could see were already dead. One of the oldest had collapsed, taking several floors with it. The factory had many more wings and many more floors, still standing defiantly, and the battle would be raging long after Garnas died.

The rubble pile formed a ramp, of sorts, leading up into the building. Garnas squinted, trying to see if the missing people had left any sign of their passage. In coming this far they were already in a great deal of trouble, but they almost certainly didn't know it. *He* was in a great deal of trouble, too, but his eyes were open.

They could have gone in one of three directions. The safest way would be to go into the jungle; the factories discouraged predators. Continuing the journey along the river bank would be free of animals but the footing was uncertain. The river was sluggish and turbid and it was all too easy to get confused about which way was up if you fell in. In an emergency, however, you could let the current carry you back to town, safe from whatever might attack you. You only had to worry about what poisons you might have ingested.

The third direction took you into the heart of the factory.

The factory seemed the likeliest place for them to have gone. It was also the place where they would be most in need of rescue. He checked his long gun again.

His boots sounded too loud on the floor inside. The wind was muted by the walls, but the concrete amplified any sound he made. When he couldn't avoid stepping on the metal grilles they creaked alarmingly. There was no way to tell which would take his weight, and which would part under him, and he could not afford to give them the attention they required. That was why you always took at least four people into a factory. Two to test the way. Two to... watch.

Factory One was most familiar to him, though. He picked his way between hulking, dead machines. Pumps, presses and conveyor belts all looked alike when adorned with that much rust. One or two had fallen through the floor to smash on the ground. Their remains stood up at odd angles, strangely reminiscent of the graveyard on the coast.

Garnas could feel his back slick with moisture. Whether it was his own sweat or the humidity, he couldn't tell. His bravado and certainty began to drain out of him. He'd never been alone in one of the factories before. In fact, he'd never heard of anyone coming back alive when they had been in a factory alone.

The prudent thing would be to find somewhere to hide on the outskirts of the factory. Somewhere he couldn't be easily seen, and where he could defend his space should one of the cats overcome its fear of the factory. Wait for Margha to arrive in the morning, and let her lead the rest of the search.

Something drew him on, though. No-one knew the jungle better than him. Perhaps he'd spent so much time here he could interpret its whispers as no-one else could. Almost without thinking, he helped himself to a couple of heavy coals from an overturned hopper as he passed. There was the locker where he'd found the material for his coat. And there—

His foot hung in the air. Just behind one of the smaller rust piles on the other side of the gallery, far too close for comfort, a ripple hung in the air, a dark, oily smudge of brown that danced in the breezes blowing through the glassless windows. As it moved, familiar shapes seemed to appear and vanish. A cog here, a lever there. Sharp corners and gleaming brass. A thing so insubstantial that on first encounter most people couldn't quite believe the sense of menace they felt from it.

Machine geist.

Garnas fumbled with his long gun, swapping the flechette cartridge out for one packed with flecks of mica. Metal would do no harm to a machine geist. He should have back-up;

three or four more people with their guns ready to keep the monster at bay while he reloaded. He should have an escape route marked. He should not, in fact, be anywhere near here at all.

He kept his long gun aimed as he retreated. A clean hit might slow it down enough for him to take a second shot, but no more.

A lull in the wind coincided with his foot knocking against a pile of debris. A small length of pipe rolled away from him, off the edge of the gantry, and sang a cacophony as it clattered between the supporting struts.

The machine geist *turned*, zeroed in on him instantly, and flew directly for him.

Garnas squeezed the trigger and felt the steam pressure build up in the chamber as the water met the heavy coal. The barrel spat angrily, but the rock shards fell harmlessly wide of the geist. It was rushing now, faster than a man could run, fast as nightmares, and taking on a more solid form. Garnas pulled another cartridge from his belt and slipped it into the gun, brought the weapon back up to his cheek, snatched at the trigger. He could hear every ping and whistle as the chamber came up to pressure.

The machine geist was on him, its improbably long arms reaching past the gun's muzzle, ready to tear him apart with metal claws.

The long gun spat white fire.

The machine geist was thrown backwards into a concrete pillar, torn and shrieking. It tried to reassert solidity, but folded in on itself. A thing with no body to speak of should not be able to twitch and writhe so in its death throes.

Only then did Garnas's hands begin to shake.

The echoes of the second blast returned, jarring him back to reality. The spirits of the factory would already be restless due to the disturbed weather. Now the noisy destruction of one would bring others in short order.

He could hear the slither of metal on metal all around him as geists rose out of their torpor.

The wind found fresh vigour, splashes of rain betraying the storm it had threatened. Underneath the roar, though, was another sound, one Garnas barely caught before the gale overpowered it. Voices, shouting. They were coming from above.

The summit of Factory One, like all the others, bore a large bare platform of uncertain purpose. Garnas couldn't tell if the shouting had come all the way from up there, but there was a certain inevitability about it.

He hurried to the end of the gantry and wrestled open a warped steel door. It screeched in reluctance but he was through, pulling it shut behind him before the noise drew attention from any of the geists. The space he was now in was barely a closet, dark and rank with the smell of stagnant water. He adjusted the strap of his long gun so it hung across his back and reached gingerly out until he found the ladder.

The builders of the factory had shown foresight in making this ladder out of a superior grade of steel, one that was faring better against the ravages of time. One day it would succumb, as it all must. Garnas hoped he wasn't halfway up it when it did.

He climbed carefully, feeling for each rung as he went. There were other stairs and ladders, but none in such good condition and none that connected with so many of the factory's floors. Every so often he passed one of them. The doors were all shut tight to keep the geists out, a precaution anyone familiar with the jungle would be sure to take. Far above, though, a tell-tale square of light said one of them was open. More evidence of the lost adventurers.

From time to time the wind would gust at just the right angle to resonate with the air in the ladder shaft, creating a rapid thud-thud-thud that made Garnas's ears pop until the direction changed again.

He resisted the urge to hurry. Anything could await him at the top and he needed to be ready to fight—or run.

It became clear that the only open door was the very top hatch. They had had the sense to close whichever door they had used to access the ladder.

Garnas had his eyes narrowed almost to slits when he peered out onto the platform. The wind whipped the hood off his head. Fat raindrops hammered down in waves on the stained concrete. Even the most belligerent vines hadn't reached so high. Seeing no immediate threat, Garnas clambered onto the great, flat expanse and swung his long gun back into position.

The view from the top was amazing. The fat, brown snake of the river stood out against the rolling layers of green that ran all the way to the horizon. Garnas counted the other factories as they followed the river's path further inland. Factory Two, Factory Three. Factory Four had collapsed entirely. The rain made it hard to make out, but the distant shadow that looked like a hill was actually Factory Seven, the largest one found, easily ten times the size of Factory One. Somewhere upriver there must be the last factory, Garnas thought, far further than anyone had dared to venture, and upstream of there it could only be assumed the water ran clear and pure.

Some distance across the platform was an old corrugated iron hut. Garnas thought he saw movement through one of the little windows. A splash of blue colour, clearly something alien to this place.

He waved an arm high in greeting, trying to attract attention. When he saw more movement through the window, he made as big a beckoning gesture as he could.

The door to the shack opened and two people peered out, looking dubiously at the heavy rain.

The first wore an outfit of dyed leather, mostly dark green but with splashes of lighter green and yellow. The shape suggested it was for protection rather than fashion. Her hair was tied back in a practical bun and a heavy axe hung from a loop on her belt.

The second wore the blue Garnas had seen, a long tunic, missing a sleeve, over light grey breeches and a vest. His hair was long and whipped across his face. He carried no weapons. A scholar travelling with a bodyguard, Garnas assumed.

They hesitated. Garnas beckoned again, more forcefully.

He was relieved to see them step out from their shelter and start jogging towards him. The platform was turning a darker colour as the rain began to soak into it. Garnas, not quite realising what he saw at first, saw the place where the surface was still dry and pale.

When he traced the shape of it his blood ran cold. He sprinted towards the others, waving his arms, trying to get them to change direction. His long gun swung in front of him and nearly tripped him over.

The texture of the air changed. Random wisps of smoke coalesced. A long, deep scratch appeared in the floor. The damp air smelled of burning oil. Above the patch of dry concrete, a monstrous figure began to appear.

The woman with the axe saw it, and lunged, tackling her companion to the ground as a massive hand swatted at where they had been. Garnas dodged out of the way as a foot made out of jagged metal shards longer than he was tall slammed down. He kept rolling, anticipating another foot, perhaps another swipe of claws.

As he regained his feet he could see the machine geist was larger by far than any he'd encountered before. He made out the shapes of multiple turbines in its body. Its arms, all three of them, looked to be cranes. Were it fully corporeal, it would have been heavy enough to break the platform in two. Broken caterpillar tracks dangled from its back.

In avoiding its blows, they had let it get between them and the hatch.

One of the caterpillar tracks lashed out. The woman took the blow on the haft of her axe and was pushed backwards a full ten feet. She adjusted her grip and ducked in to hack at one of the translucent legs.

"Metal can't harm it!" Garnas tried to shout a warning, but the storm was too fierce.

The axe only made it angrier.

The man in blue was shouting as well. Garnas could see his lips moving.

The next blow came from the side. She paid it no attention. Feet from her, it hit an invisible barrier, creating a shower of hot sparks and metal fragments. The man staggered, shook himself, and started shouting again.

If they could fight, there was hope. Garnas could scarcely miss a target that large. He let the pressure build in his gun as he ran to flank the geist. The timing was perfect for the blast to catch a caterpillar track. The cobweb remains of it were whisked into the sky by the wind and lost.

He slammed the next cartridge in by feel alone, already running. The spectre must have had a dim awareness that its prey was trying to flee. It swayed, standing directly over the hatch.

Garnas fired off a few more shots, gouging holes in the monster's semi-corporeal body but doing little other than slowing it down. He threw himself flat to avoid a sweeping paw, one that connected with the shack the wanderers had been sheltering in and sent the entire structure corkscrewing out over the jungle.

It was clear he didn't have enough ammunition to deal with the beast, even if it stood still and waited for him to shoot it. He could keep it distracted, keep it reeling, but eventually it would hit him. and that would be that.

The man was purple from the effort of shouting. The woman, in a moment of respite, held up her axe, and a tongue of dark fire leapt from him to the weapon. Now when she swung at the geist it was marginally effective. The geists were twisted memories of iron, steam and oil. Fire hurt them only a little.

In the next lull she leaned in close to the shouting man and bellowed something in his ear. Garnas hoped they were coming up with a plan, because the only one he had was to take a flying leap off the platform and hope he landed on water rather than concrete.

The next time he pulled the trigger, he felt nothing. The rain, coming at them sideways, had got into the firebox and extinguished the coal. He instinctively reached for the knife at his belt, then stopped. It would do him no good. Seeing him in difficulty, the woman gestured for him to get behind her.

She was holding her own now, just about, adapting to the machine geist's speed and rhythm. But holding her own didn't get them any closer to safety.

The man in blue was shouting again, veins standing out on his neck from the effort. Slowly, his voice got louder, supernaturally amplified. He was, Garnas realised, singing. His voice became louder than the gale, louder than the hiss of rain on leaves. He was singing to the sky.

The sky began to sing back.

It was noise Garnas felt as much as he heard. Something had been awakened in the clouds, something that had heeded the singer's call and joined him in a harmony that connected to the roots of the soul.

Clouds rushed together above them, drawn by the song. In the centre of the maelstrom a darkness grew. Garnas felt pressure build in his ears until the pain was intolerable.

When the lightning came, it was a fat bolt that struck square in the centre of the machine geist then fractured outwards in a dozen jagged forks. The geist evaporated as the thunder echoed back to them.

The moment of violence made the storm pause. The old eye collapsed and a new one was forced into existence above the factory. There was blissful quiet. Even the rain was taking a breath.

#

"How is he?"

The town opened its shutters now the rain had passed. Garnas lingered under a lean-to roof while Persinian talked to the captain, some distance away. The crew of the ship respected the elder's wish that they not venture off the dock into the town. The woman with the axe, Shirin, evidently did not care about the old man's edict. It seemed to be accepted, by all parties, that successfully returning from the jungle conferred certain privileges.

"He'll recover," she said. "He'll mither for *days*, but there's no lasting harm done. He just tired himself out."

It had been a tricky business helping her companion down the ladder. Garnas had led them a few minutes down-river where he knew a bivouac lay. He and Shirin took turns on watch, making sure none of the jungle beasts took too great an interest in the little camp, but it had been built with materials salvaged from the factory so they kept their distance. Margha's rescue party found them there early in the morning, as the rain was easing up, and the eight of them had made it back to the village in good time. Shirin and Eilert—the singer—had returned to the ship straight away, Shirin emerging again a couple of hours later. Now she loitered just close enough to listen in on Persinian's conversation. When Garnas had arrived, after catching up on some of his sleep, she wandered over to him.

Garnas smiled.

"Technically, you're both considered 'rangers' now," he said. "Because you came back."

She laughed.

"I learned two things yesterday. The first is a healthy respect for the wilderness here. The second is: never let Eilert talk me into anything."

"I guess you'll be leaving with the ship?"

"Aye. We don't like to linger."

"You've travelled a lot?"

"Not as much as some, but more than most."

"You'll have seen some incredible places, then. I guess this place must be nothing special."

"Everywhere is special," she said, quickly. "I've never seen somewhere like here before, and I doubt I will again."

They watched the captain and Persinian talking. The wind was fresh. The storm had spent its energies and left behind a feeling of renewal.

"You won't come back here?"

Shirin shrugged.

"I can't rule it out. We go where fate takes us. But probably not."

"But you could, if you wanted to?"

"Sure. Valexia is the only captain I know with a rutter for this town, though. It took a while to find a ship to get us here, but once we heard about this place we wanted to see it."

She looked out to sea, where the stain of the river's outflow swirled gently.

"It was worth the effort. Although not the danger we put ourselves in."

She started to say something else, but stopped.

Garnas knew what she was thinking. Gratitude for being rescued didn't need to be expressed between equals. They were both seasoned fighters and scouts, even if her own experience had not properly prepared her for the jungle. He realised that his own experience must be similarly limited; in fact dramatically moreso.

The seagulls circled in the skies up the coast, fishing. Garnas realised he felt no urge to do the same.

"This captain," he said. "The ship. Is there room for one more passenger?"

"I believe so. We've been such good customers for Valexia that I could probably persuade her to waive your fare. But you seem very much at home here. You really want to leave?"

Garnas fingered the hem of his coat.

"I've been waiting for someone. For a long time. But I realise now they'll probably never come."

He looked to the north, past the seagulls, to the hazy coastline beyond the headland.

"I've exhausted what I can do here. When I come back, it'll be because I've made certain there's nowhere else I belong more."

Shirin grabbed his forearm and pulled him towards the ship.

"Come on, then. No time like the present. Valexia always wants to leave with the tide. Eilert will be unhappy, though."

"Why?"
"He just lost a bet."

The Shaved Link

Shirin ran the whetstone along the edge of her axe. The scrape was so familiar she barely heard it. The sailors had given her some good-natured ribbing about it—"If you keep sharpening it there'll be no blade left!"—until she'd told them it was a ritual. The rough men and women of the sea might have limited respect for non-sailors, but ritual was central to a lot of what they did. Seas were capricious. No-one wanted to tempt fate. In a way, it *was* a ritual, albeit one with a purpose. The axe was special, although nobody on the ship but her knew how special.

It was hungry for metal. When it struck armour, it bit far deeper than its edge and weight alone could manage. The axe's hunger was unceasing, drinking in motes of iron from any object around it. If it was kept in a metal crate, then after a month there would be precious little of the crate left, and the axe head would be a misshapen mass too heavy to wield. So Shirin attended to it three times a day: first the rasp, then the whetstone. Morning, noon, and evening. A ritual, indeed.

When she was happy with the edge and shape of the curve, she wrapped the whetstone up and returned it to her luggage. She slipped the axe into the loop at her belt and tied the leather cover over the head, returning to awareness of the sounds around her. The creak of the ship's timbers, the hammock swinging in the adjacent room, muffled shouting as the crew called to each other. Even the brash calls of seagulls.

She stood up. Captain Valexia always insisted Shirin share her cabin when she travelled on the *Shaved Link*. At first, the axe-woman had concerns as to the captain's intentions, but the truth of the matter was Valexia took special care of any woman who came aboard the *Shaved Link*. Special consideration was given to women in traditionally male occupations, on the basis that they would probably appreciate a reprieve from having to prove themselves over and over to their colleagues.

However, Valexia wasn't keen on taking any passenger on board if she didn't think they could pull their weight. She had reason to be cautious, given her history. The *Shaved Link* was not a ship you could charter at any price. If a trusted connection introduced you to Valexia, on the other hand, a small consideration would get you taken on as a passenger, and with a little more you could nominate the next port it visited. Unlike the huge cargo vessels that dominated trade, the small barque carried a variety of goods and could do business just about anywhere. This was how Shirin and Eilert had arranged passage to their most recent destination, a trip rather more eventful than anyone had liked.

#

Loss Report Summary

The fullest accounting of what happened to the Silver Locket and the balance of her crew comes from the second mate, whose testimony is supported by those other crew that escaped the catastrophe. The ship anchored off the coast of Van'sleh, as was customary, as there is no harbour of suitable size for such a large ship. Boats were sent ashore with goods, under the command of the second mate, to finalise sale at the agreed price. While unloading the cargo, a storm sprang up. It was adjudged too dangerous to return to the ship, so the crew ashore remained there. The ship moved further away from the coast, for safety, then dropped anchor again. Come the morning, the Silver Locket had vanished with all the crew aboard it. We anticipate that this state of affairs will cause much difficulty with the insurers.

#

Shirin was able to enjoy the relative luxury of the captain's cabin, but Eilert had been consigned to a hammock like the rest of the crew.

He looked up when Shirin emerged from the cabin.

"How are you feeling today?" she asked.

He flicked his notebook to its last page and pointed to one of the phrases he'd written there: 'Getting better'. She knew little about the arcane art of the cantors, but he'd made it clear the effort expended at the factory had hurt his throat. It made sense to Shirin that controlling energies of that magnitude could have debilitating costs. She knew some of the sailors believed he was exaggerating his condition, in order to avoid helping out on the ship, but in all the time she'd known him he'd never been dishonest with her. If he didn't feel ready to speak yet, she didn't intend to make him. It had only been three days, after all.

Her other travelling companion was up on deck again. Or, more likely, hanging over the rail.

Garnas looked up when Shirin approached. He was as pale as ever. He hadn't been able to keep a single morsel of food down and the bags under his eyes suggested he was just as deprived of sleep. He looked in a worse way than Eilert.

"I think I'm managing somewhat better," he declared, in defiance of the evidence of her eyes.

"Maybe the sailors have something to help?" she asked.

He shook his head.

"They said not. Apparently I just need to acclimatise?" He tried to sound confident, but it came across as more of a question.

She put a pitying hand on his shoulder, then pulled it back when he turned back to the sea and retched again.

Shirin sought out the quartermaster, Tasset, a surly old salt who doled out water and food as though he was parting with his own fingers. Any free moment he had was spent below decks working at his scrimshaw, and such was his skill he probably could have given up on the sea and made a living with his art—but one look at him was enough to tell anyone not only that he lived on the sea, but that he would die and be buried there, too.

"Can I buy some tar kelp?" she asked him. "My bag got ruined in the jungle."

"Sure thing, miss."

Shirin had found it hard to take against his use of 'miss'. He seemed to consider it a polite honorific and used it with any woman, even his captain. He opened a supply chest, pulled out a small waxed pouch and passed it to her. Shirin counted out the right coins and he palmed them with a nod.

"A bit extra in there for you, miss. To make up for the trouble ashore."

"Thanks, it's very thoughtful of you." She was especially polite, hoping to minimise any awkwardness should he discover her deceit.

She took the pouch straight to Garnas and pressed it into his hand, out of sight of the sailors.

"Chew a pinch of this. It'll settle your stomach."

He opened it, sniffed, and pulled a face.

"I know," she said. "But it does the trick."

He gave her a look as though he suspected a prank. There *was* a prank involved, but not from her. Getting riotously ill was considered a rite of passage and it was traditional for new crew to be kept uninformed about the remedy. Shirin detested that sort of behaviour, but it wasn't her place to take them to task about it.

"I think I'm mostly over it," Garnas said.

Shirin shook her head.

"It's going to get much worse from tomorrow," she told him. "Trust me."

He reached in the bag, extracted some of the dark green powder, and gingerly pushed it into his mouth.

"You get used to the taste, right?"

She chuckled.

"People keep telling me so. I'm not convinced."

It was probably her imagination, but Garnas looked a little better immediately. She clapped him on the shoulder. With luck he'd be able to enjoy the view by the afternoon. Looking straight down didn't do the ocean justice.

#

Internal Memo

The loss of that damned ship will hit us hard. Finally reached a provisional agreement with the insurers for far less than I wanted. The rest of the board got cold feet. Cowards. We should recoup the cost of the lost cargo in full but obtaining a replacement vessel will be beyond our present cash reserves. Every day that passes is lost revenue from the route. We may have to liquidate some of our investments and eat one loss just to avoid a greater one. Fortunately the bereavement payouts to the families are at the very low end—or even below it—so it's not as bad as it could be. The money from the cargo that was sold before the disaster will help. The second mate is travelling with it on the Pewter Locket *and it should be in our coffers by the middle of next week.*

#

Captain Valexia appeared on the quarterdeck and beckoned Shirin over. Two of the ship's three navigators were with her. They'd left their charts below and were comparing pages from tattered note books. The captain was all smiles, as usual. If Shirin hadn't also seen her full of fury, when necessary, she would have struggled to believe it was possible.

"We're on target to flip mid-afternoon," Valexia announced. "Are you happy to take care of your companions? Eilert is still poorly, and as for the greenhorn, well..."

"He should be recovering soon." She was about to say more but stopped herself. She didn't want to give away that she'd undermined his hazing.

"Ordinarily I'd have no issue with you being on deck for the transition—you've been through enough of them—but you'll need to keep them both safe."

"Absolutely. I hadn't thought about it but it's obvious."

"Good, good. I just wanted to make sure there was no confusion." The captain turned to leave, but paused. "Don't let Eilert hog the porthole. The new chap should get the best view."

Shirin doubted the cantor would want to leave his sick bed, even to watch a transition, but it wouldn't be altogether out of character for him to rapidly and suspiciously rally so he could enjoy the spectacle. The captain left and the navigators trailed after her, arguing about the precise location of the transition. It seemed a moot point to Shirin. It was hardly going to be difficult to find.

The quartermaster had been standing a short distance behind the captain and was revealed when she stepped away. The point of his knife picked at the ivory in his other hand. There was the mere suggestion of a smile on his craggy old features; a twinkle in the eyes underneath his heavy brows.

The wily old buzzard knew what I was doing, Shirin thought. *That's why he gave me a bit extra.*

She went back to lean on the rail next to Garnas, and they watched the sea roll by in silence. One of the purest joys of travel was to be with a companion, not saying anything, not doing anything, just being in the process of moving from place to place. She would have preferred to do so with Eilert, but Garnas would do. She might have known him for less than a week, but spending one fraught night in a cramped bivouac, alert for attacks by large predators, tended to accelerate the development of camaraderie.

Noon passed, remarked only by a whistle to indicate the change of watch. When the crew hauled on ropes to reef the sail, Shirin nudged Garnas.

"We should get below. We're going to flip soon."

"Going to... what?"

"'Flip'. The ship will make a transition soon."

"Transition?"

She looked at him incredulously for a moment, then realised he really didn't know about flips or any other kind of transition or, indeed, about the interstice at all. He had truly led a sheltered life. The headman of his village—Shirin forgot his name—was fully aware of the particulars of deep sailing but evidently it was a closed book to anyone else there. She thought it strangely incurious of them.

"It will make sense afterwards, trust me. But we'll just be in the sailors' way if we stay up here."

He followed her down the ladder and into the general quarters. They squeezed past sailors coming the other way; both watches were needed for the manoeuvre.

Eilert was leaning over the side of his hammock, his fingertips touching a rope on the floor but not quite able to grasp it. He knew how to prepare for what was coming. Shirin, feeling unpleasantly matronly, took the rope and made the side of the hammock secure to make sure Eilert wouldn't spill out. She told Garnas to tuck in against the wall, by the porthole, and showed him where other lengths of rope could be tied through his belt loops. He must have looked trepidatious at all the preparation, so Shirin gave him a reassuring wink as she made herself fast the other side of the hammock.

"This is really just a precaution," she told him.

Eilert caught her glance and rolled his eyes. He scribbled something in the back of his notebook and thrust it in front of Garnas.

"It's rough but safe."

"You'll want to watch this," Shirin added, and gestured to the window.

The ship had lost speed with its reduced sail and the sea still looked to be flat calm, almost glass-like in the distance. Garnas was clearly confused as to how such a tranquil vista could become rough.

Shirin heard him gasp as the whirlpool came into view. The ship accelerated as it passed, caught in the outer reaches of the vortex, then heeled as it turned towards it. Garnas leaned to one side, trying to keep it in his restricted field of vision but also looking alarmed to see they were turning towards it rather than away. The *Shaved Link* rode the current, faster and faster, until it was taken into the funnel. The rudder was hard over, fighting the ship's tendency to point straight down into the abyss. They stared at the roaring wall of water that made up the opposite side, at a distance less than twice the height of the main mast. Shirin felt her stomach lurch. Speed kept the ship against the water and stopped it from simply dropping sideways. The mismatch between what she saw and what she felt couldn't be ignored. Garnas took a generous pinch of tar kelp. He had gone pale. Eilert swung gently in his hammock, an unwilling plumb bob.

They remained in limbo for what felt like an age. The *Shaved Link* spiralled into the maelstrom, each orbit slighter deeper, slightly faster.

At the bottom of the whirlpool there was only darkness, total and featureless. Not the green pelagic gloom of the deep sea, or the brown and grey of the sea floor, but the absolute black that mocked all attempts to cast light into it. It was unnatural and threatening. The ship had heeled so far the porthole looked directly down. There was something wrong with gravity. Centrifugal force alone could not explain why the floor still felt as though it was underneath them.

Somewhere up on deck a signal was given. The rudder went from one extreme to the other, pointing the ship straight down with a judder that made every timber creak in protest. Then the wheel was released and the rudder allowed to dictate its own angle as the ship plunged onward.

Garnas was transfixed by the droplets of water hanging in the air outside the porthole. Those drops—and the ship— were in freefall. Then, impossibly, the droplets fell astern as the ship out-paced them.

Blackness.

Then they stared out into a dark sky, pierced with vivid points of light. Garnas let out his breath tumble out of him loudly. The other two let theirs out more measuredly. Shirin left him staring in wonder as she untied all the ropes.

"Well, that's what a transition is," she said. "A type of 'flip' specifically. Come on, you'll like the view from up on deck."

She could barely keep up with him as he hurried up the ladder.

Once on deck he stared into the sky, head thrown fully back. He bounced off one sailor, then another, oblivious to his surroundings. Shirin gently led him to one side so he didn't get in the way any more than necessary.

She watched expression of wonder turned to puzzlement. He scanned the sky methodically, looking for constellations he knew. When he couldn't find them, he looked to the ship's horizon, maybe trying to find specific stars. There would be nothing familiar in any direction he looked.

Shirin waited for him to notice that the stars were underneath the ship, too. They weren't true stars, but she didn't want to ruin the moment by telling him.

"I... see," he said, eventually. "I didn't realise anything like this existed."

"In some places the interstice is a closely-guarded secret. In others, it's just another way to travel."

The sailors let out the sails and they caught a wind that came from nowhere and blew to nowhere.

"So this place is like a shortcut? Taking us back to the sea in another part of the world?"

Shirin chose her words carefully. It could be a lot to take in all at once. The crew hadn't exactly treated him badly, but their perception of him was as dead weight and that would only intensify if he handled the interstice badly.

"No, not another part of the world. Think of the land and the sea together as being one shore. This is the ocean between many of those shores. Every point of light you see around us is its own world, more or less."

He stared up in wonder. Struck by a thought, he turned and looked directly aft. There wasn't much to see. One of the points of light was clearly larger than the others, but it was just as featureless.

"Your world is harder to reach than most," Shirin explained. "It can't be seen very well, even from here."

Reflected light danced in his eyes. This was why she liked to travel in company. To experience wonders through another's eyes was as good as seeing them for the first time herself. Garnas turned back to the sky. Lace ribbons criss-crossed everywhere, in all the colours.

"So many..."

TO SAIL THE INTERSTICE

#

Marine Investigator's Report

Examination of the area by local divers discovered the anchor, still at rest on the sea bed. Approximately four feet of chain remains attached. A single fractured link matching the rest of the chain was also found. This is highly suggestive of an anchor chain failure. It's unknown what action the captain took in response, if any. It is hypothesised that the ship was, by chance, drawn to the transition point it had entered by, and such an unprepared transition left it wrecked in the interstice, but this cannot be proven. Experiments with buoys have been unable to recreate the event. People in the area cannot recall a similar incident happening before, but vouchsafe that wrecks and losses in general occur seldom there.

#

Garnas had recovered somewhat the next day and he rose early. Shirin found him in the chart room, talking to one of the navigators.

"A rutter is more 'n a chart. A chart will tell you where things are, what you can see when you're some ways off'f the coast. You can pinpoint exactly where you are on a chart, but that ain't the full story. A rutter is better 'n that. It's got notes. It tells you, step by step, exac'ly what you need to do to get where you're goin'."

"Things like... sand bars and reefs?" Garnas asked.

"Aye. And other things. Currents is a big one. Like fer your town, this told me to approach from along the coast rather than sailin' straight fer it. The river water comes out fast an' it's got stuff in as can scour the hull. Damage it, even."

They hadn't noticed Shirin come in. She didn't want to disturb them and potentially interrupt a rare moment where one of the crew was bonding with the newcomer.

"Are you making a copy?"

"Ev'ry navigator has 'is own rutter. 'Tis the symbol of the trade, the bigger the better. This rutter belongs to the cap'n, acquired with the ship. I get to make a copy of this page for making the trip. That's how it works. I also updates or corrects as needed."

"Like adding in the fallen crane?"

"Aye."

"But why two copies?"

"One fer me, one fer the old rutter. I won't deface the original, just paste this page in next to it."

Garnas watched the navigator work for a minute or two. Each page was a fold-out history past journeys. The job needed someone who was a draughtsman as well as a mathematician.

"Why does it stop here and here?"

"Nobody in this lineage of rutters has sailed s'far along the coast."

"I could fill it in."

When the navigator looked unconvinced, Garnas continued: "I've been walking up and down that coast for twenty years. It would be a poor show if I couldn't sketch it from memory."

The navigator pushed the half-finished copy over to Garnas and furnished him with a pencil. As Garnas worked, the navigator looked up and saw Shirin loitering near the door. She didn't want either of them to feel ill at ease so she pointed to the broken chain link fixed to the far wall.

"While he works on it, why not tell him how the ship got its name?"

"Ah, well—"

#

Personal Correspondence

I'm just as angry as you are, S, but we're limited in what we can do. We can hardly send people round to widows' houses and demand the money back. We might have legal standing but the backlash would ruin us as a company. The same goes for prosecuting V—we'd be branded as the company that sues people who try to do right by their crews. I've spoken to B and he agrees our best course of action is to turn it to our advantage. The low payout to the families caused some discontent and we can pretend that using the cargo money to increase it was our idea. I agree V shouldn't be allowed to get away with it, though—'one good turn deserves another'. She's finished with our company. A few words in the right ears and no other company will take her on. They'll stand with us on this, I'm sure. Nobody wants this sort of behaviour to set a precedent.

#

The version of the story the navigator told was considerably embellished from the one Shirin had heard from Captain Valexia herself; it even added two sea monsters.

Garnas had finished drawing by then. The navigator reached for the pantograph and prepared to make a copy.

"O' course," he added, "the real value in a rutter is in the pages for the interstice. Without *those* directions you won't even be able to follow the safe channels. And as fer finding the right spot for a transition—"

He was interrupted by shouting on deck. A whistle sounded and Shirin's blood ran cold. She pulled Garnas aside while the navigator hurriedly stowed everything on the table.

"This could be bad. We're under attack."

She watched the shock play out on his face and used the time to evaluate her next step. There was plenty she could do to help repel any boarders, but until the enemy was close enough to hit she was useless. The important part of the battle would come before then. Attackers seldom came within boarding distance unless they were confident they could overwhelm the target—either by force of numbers or by giving them such a pounding from cannon that they couldn't put up much of a fight. Without a word she bundled Garnas out of the room and back down between the rows of hammocks.

Eilert was sitting up, alert.

"Can you sing?" Shirin asked him, without preamble.

He opened his mouth but only a croaking noise came out. He shook his head.

Garnas pulled his travelling trunk out from under a shelf and opened it. His long gun was stored in three parts and he started fitting them together immediately. Shirin looked at it doubtfully. It was a big weapon, barely man-portable, designed for wounding or scaring away large animals. It was unsuited to dealing with smaller, more nimble targets at close quarters.

"We stay here for now. We'd just be extra targets on deck." Her tone made it clear she was just as unhappy about that as Garnas evidently was.

They listened to the shouting. There were more whistles, and a sense of haste and panic filtered through the boards of the deck.

Eilert coughed and pointed urgently through the port-hole.

There was another ship visible, one rising up to meet the *Shaved Link* from below. Shirin knew that wasn't good. It took specialised equipment to be able to fire at targets directly below them, equipment that Valexia's ship, as a small trader, didn't carry. From the size of the enemy ship, Shirin's help wouldn't be enough to turn the tide once the grapples were thrown across.

The enemy ship was rising sharply. Cannons spoke on both sides and the splintering of wood was nearly as loud. Shirin guessed they would come to a halt above the *Shaved Link*, at too high an angle to be hit by cannons. If Eilert was at the peak of his powers, they could probably create a stand-off, but as things stood...

"Does this thing open?" Garnas asked, running his fingers around the edge of the porthole.

Shirin helped him with the wing nuts. The noise was much louder once the brass frame swung aside. Garnas opened a hatch in the side of his weapon and poked a slow-burning match inside. He blew gently through the opening until he appeared satisfied. Just before the enemy brigantine drew to the same altitude, he poked the barrel of his gun through the port, and pulled the trigger.

A blast of metal fragments erupted from the end of the muzzle and tore into the approaching ship's sails. The rigging was thrown into disarray. The enemy buccaneers yelled in shock, but it was too late for them to see exactly where the shot had come from.

Garnas was already replacing the spent cartridge.

"You can't sink a ship in the interstice," Shirin pointed out. "They can take all the time they want repairing the hull."

"If they intercepted us," Garnas replied, staring down the sights, "they were either faster than us, or between us and our destination. I reckon if we damage their ship enough, we can outrun them for long enough to reach safety." He narrowed his eyes as the brigantine's rudder came into view. "There we go."

The shot he fired was a solid ball that shattered the strong wood of the rudder with a single blow. Battle had been joined on the deck above, bloody and chaotic.

"One more," Garnas said, selecting a third cartridge.

#

Marine Investigator's Addendum

Examination of the Silver Locket's *sister vessel, the* Pewter Locket, *revealed a design flaw in the capstan assembly. The grommet the anchor chain passes through is placed too high, and has too sharp an edge. The* Pewter Locket's *own anchor chain showed serious signs of abrasion. Discussion with that ship's captain revealed that regular inspections of the anchor chain were discouraged by the Company as unnecessary, as the anchor only needed to be used at one destination in the* Silver Locket's *regular route. We make a strong recommendation that regular inspections be required on all vessels in the fleet, and that the grommets be replaced and repositioned on affected ships as soon as is practical.*

#

Climbing a ladder would have been too dangerous, so Shirin took a detour to come out on deck through a door. She emerged directly behind an enemy and a single smooth axe strike almost severed his neck. As he fell, another attacker thrust a cutlass at her. She dodged it easily, bringing her axe down on his shoulder. It glided through his pauldron as though through cloth. The pirate ship loomed large and threatening over the *Shaved Link*. Grapples were thrown over the latter's rail to bind the two vessels together. Wave after wave of attackers leapt into the fray.

She ran over to where the captain barked out desperate orders. Valexia acknowledged her with a nod. Shirin leaned in close to shout the good news.

"We've crippled their ship! If we break free we can escape!"

"How crippled?" Valexia demanded.

Before Shirin could answer, a bloom of fire erupted around the aft of the brigantine. The bright yellow colour and the way it clung to the hull suggested it was fuelled by incendiary chemicals.

Shirin dashed off towards the nearest line, trying to plan a route where she could cut as many as possible without getting surrounded. Behind her, Captain Valexia blew a short sequence of notes on her whistle. At the for'ard end of the deck, one of the crew swung a boarding axe and chopped through the end of the rail. As it swung free, Shirin whipped her head around to see the aft end had been cut as well. The entire rail pulled free of the *Shaved Link* and took all the boarding lines with it. The ships began to separate.

Many of the attackers, seeing how things were likely to play out, dropped their weapons and jumped, reaching to grasp the rail, or even just someone else's leg. A few didn't make it, and fell into the emptiness of the interstice with despairing screams.

The sails of the *Shaved Link* dropped open all at once, courtesy of more boarding axes, and the ship picked up speed.

The pirate brigantine made no attempt to pursue. Neither did any of its cannons fire. Combating the sticky fire appeared to occupy all of her crew's efforts.

Despite the odds, the *Shaved Link* had escaped.

#

Hepatizon Coast Newsletter Excerpt

The story of the loss of the Silver Locket *(thought to be at its conclusion last year) has received an addendum. The ship's second mate, who regular readers will remember is called Valexia, was the beneficiary of an unexpected windfall in the form of a large monetary gift. Apparently one of the lost sailors was a cousin of a rich family (although your reporter has not been able to discover which one) and they were so moved by the second mate's gesture (the money being but a pittance to them) that they rewarded her with a substantial sum. In maritime affairs, it seems, one good turn deserves another.*

She has voiced her intention to buy her own ship, to be run as an independent courier. History will show whether her captaincy will be as ill-starred as her last post (although we all earnestly hope not). A broken piece of anchor chain (a keepsake she kept from the catastrophe) will give the new vessel its name: the Shaved Link. *The newly-minted captain intends to enplaque the memento and display it prominently. She told your reporter: "A ship's crew is like a chain. It only takes one weak member for it to fail.". Here's hoping she can find sufficient sailors of the calibre she requires.*

#

There were a handful of boarders stranded on the *Shaved Link* as it sped away. The crew made sure they were disarmed and marched them into a group.

Shirin took in their tattered clothes and how spare around the ribs they were. Unwilling conscripts or desperate men, plainly. There was precious little fight left in them.

Valexia made sure she had their full attention before speaking.

"It looks like hard luck has come your way recently, and you have my sympathy. But I won't have you staying on this ship, not after what you tried to do to me and mine. Once we reach port you can either look for honest work there, or if you're wanted by the authorities I'll give you a running start. It's the best offer you're going to get, so don't cut up rough. Until we get there you'll be in the hold, in irons. You'll get proper rations."

Once the prisoners had been taken below, Valexia allowed herself a sigh of relief. The deck was still full of people. Even those not actively sailing the ship and dressing wounds were milling about. Nervous energy was everywhere after the narrow escape.

"That was a clever idea with the rail," Shirin said, somewhat louder than necessary. She'd seen enough bloodshed to know when the tension needed to be let out amongst the survivors. Anything to occupy their minds, stop them dwelling on what had just happened, and what had just been avoided.

"I can't take credit for that trick," Valexia said. "I heard about someone trying it a couple of years ago. Take out most of the rail struts before the enemy closes the gap. On a ship like this there's not much else for the grapples get hold of. If you cut it free you can run—assuming you are faster than the enemy. Remind me to thank Eilert for so magnificently changing their priorities."

"Actually, you should thank Garnas. Apparently he had an incendiary shell for that gun of his."

Valexia looked taken aback. Garnas was up on deck, without his weapon now, and she allowed herself a glance in his direction.

"Those things are *dangerous*. If I'd known he'd brought one aboard I would have made him throw it over the side." She thought for a moment. "Which would have been a terrible mistake, apparently."

"If we'd thought about it we'd have realised he's basically hauling around his own swivel gun."

They watched him help a wounded sailor down some steps. Shirin wasn't sure if it was her imagination or not, but the crew seemed to be treating Garnas a little differently. He'd been a passenger, a *tourist* up until now. An obstacle to the smooth running of the ship. Now he was accepted.

Shirin hadn't been through a rite of passage like that. Her reputation had preceded her onto the *Shaved Link*.

Captain Valexia coughed, breaking Shirin out of her reverie.

"We found this on one of the prisoners."

She handed over a printed note so thin and worn its creases were coming apart of their own accord. Shirin gingerly opened it. Her expression hardened as she read it. It announced a reward for the live capture of the thief and traitor, Shirin of the Locked Tower.

"You're in no danger from anyone on this ship," Valexia said, "You have my word. However, we'll have to part ways when we arrive at port. Nothing personal, but it's too big a risk. For all we know those pirates came looking for you specifically."

"I understand," Shirin said, suppressing a far more bitter response.

She'd dared to hope that the past wasn't going to catch up with her. It had been nearly a year since her first desperate flight from home. Falling in with Eilert had made things easier. He accepted the risk, even when she'd refused to explain the circumstances. The cantor was generous of spirit to a fault. He'd stick with her. Garnas, though, did not deserve to be left to fend for himself and she knew of no-one she could trust to take him under their wing in her stead. What was best for him? To carry on helping him adjust to his new life, or to put him out of the danger she brought? She could flee as much as she wanted but the past was always chasing. If the running became the ritual, what else would be left in her life?

BEN WRIGHT

The Hepatizon Coast

The mist caressed Garnas's face like a lover. Gone were
the days of wretched illness and self-pity. He stared out
over the interstice with what he believed was the gaze of an
old salt. Somewhere below, the ship's great brass gyroscope
hummed on its axle. Captain Valexia called down a speaking
tube and answering shouts confirmed that cranks were being
turned the requested number of revolutions. The pinprick
sky shifted slowly above them as the *Shaved Link* adjusted its
roll.

The lights in the sky were fainter now. Were there fewer
than there had been a minute ago? Garnas couldn't tell. He
turned and looked ahead, to where a vast marble showed
him a fish-eye vision of their destination. There was water,
extensive wooden docks, and what looked like tiers of streets
on the lower slope of a bare hill. The image was too smeared
to see details, but what could be seen looked exotic to Garnas's eyes. He was used to the greens of the sea and the jungle and the thousand orange shades of rust. These piercing
swatches of colour: the blues, the whites, the yellows; they
tantalised.

Perhaps it was his imagination, but he thought he could
already hear seagulls. The interstice was untroubled by
incidental noise, which had only made the sounds of the
ship seem louder. Even the muted voices of the sailors had
become intrusive. Now the cracking of the sails rang in Garnas's ears. The whine of the gyroscope was fading.

The mist thickened. He'd been told that this transition
would be far more peaceful than the last and he was allowed
to be on deck. When the fog was so thick it hid even his companions, Garnas heard a call run up and down the deck.

"Brace!"

He wasn't sure if he was supposed to join in, but he knew to set his body against the ship's rail—on the starboard side, the port side rail was still missing—and tense.

Something struck the prow of the ship like a giant's fist, making every timber groan in protest. Even prepared as he was, Garnas nearly toppled forwards. He apologised as he pulled himself away from Shirin's back.

Waves rolled against the hull as the ship broke free of the mist. With only a single judder it had left the interstice to rejoin a mundane sea. The vision in the marble had not done the port justice. Colours were in constant motion. Shouts carried all the way out to the ship; hawkers' lures drowned out top-of-voice squabbles, pierced in turn by children's excited shrieks.

Jetty after jetty was occupied by a ship. The *Shaved Link* turned to port, looking for a vacant berth.

"They say," Eilert was standing at Garnas's shoulder, as he had been since they came up on deck, "that you used to be able to walk from one end of the docks to the other, ship to ship, never setting foot on land. Grand Billon is considered the jewel of the Hepatizon coast."

His keen eyes picked out a space and he whistled a short series of notes. The lookout, high up in the rigging, appeared to understand and looked to the same part of the docks. He repeated the whistle, confirming Eilert's discovery.

"What changed?" Garnas asked.

Eilert shrugged.

"Business decisions. Currents in the interstice. Change will always come."

The *Shaved Link* was one of the smallest ships there. She passed a galleon sitting low in the water, a junk-rigged schooner almost lost in a haze of incense smoke, and a squat, iron-clad frigate bristling with gun ports. A dock hand threw a line to the ship as it coasted up. It became clear the crew were well-practised at this manoeuvre when the ship nudged the wharf with the gentlest of kisses and came to a halt. Repairs would have to be made before she put out to sea again, but Garnas, Shirin and Eilert would not be with her. They were the first down the gangplank.

Garnas had missed gulls. There were no gulls here, he realised, but bats. Bats with slick and oily fur, as ready to dive and snatch a person's meal as to dive into the sea in search of fish. Their piping voices called back and forth and nobody paid them any mind.

There was never a time when the docks were not busy. Shirin and Eilert flanked Garnas, instinctively acting as buffers, and he was grateful. One step onto the docks and he was in the midst of more people than he had seen in his entire life. His eyes could find no purchase in the crowd, seeing but not seeing, pausing only when something caught his attention. Here was a man who was twice as tall as the rest, carrying a wooden crate on each shoulder, inching closer to his destination with a series of polite requests to make room. There was a woman with the hind-quarters of a lioness, shouting bare-chested orders in a language Garnas didn't know. By the wall of a warehouse a bald man emerged from a cloud of steam, enmeshed in an intricate steel device that did his walking for him on six cantilevered legs. From the wall of rusty cages behind him an unseen host of creatures chittered.

It would have been easy to become overwhelmed. Garnas felt the possibility in his chest, thrumming like a trapped bird. Stronger, though, was the sense of the world unfolding in front of him like a map. The intuition that if he could but find the legend to that map and unpick its secrets, nothing in the universe would be kept from him.

#

It didn't look quite like a shop, nor quite like a hotel lobby, but it did look expensive. Garnas was acutely aware of his tatty boots, still speckled with rust particles. Eilert, by contrast, drifted nonchalantly across the carpet and set his bags down by the counter.

"I understand a wayliner is leaving for the Caelum Cathedrale tomorrow. Are tickets still available?"

The woman behind the counter was, in turn, behind a small forest of levers that cordoned her off like ramparts. She took the card Eilert offered and pulled a sequence of controls with practised efficiency. Machinery hidden inside the counter jerked into noisy life.

"Welcome back, cantor. Yes, we still have tickets available in third class. How many are you looking for?"

"Three, please. Myself and two guests, one of whom needs to be registered."

"One-way, third class for three people comes to eighty-one thalers."

Her uniform matched the colours of the lobby, but the palette had been selected with such faultless good taste that the overall effect avoided being déclassé.

"Ah. It's rather more than I hoped it would be. I don't suppose there are any special discounts we could take advantage of?"

"I'm sorry, cantor."

Eilert leaned on the counter, in a way that deliberately emphasised the ceremonial blue of his clothes.

"I have always appreciated the care Starpenny Line has taken with me when I've travelled with them. To tell a secret, I'm heading home on account of a medical emergency."

The woman adopted an expression of professional concern that did not quite mask the underlying professional doubt.

Eilert held his other hand palm up and started singing softly. Delicate orange flames danced around his fingers until his voice cracked and the fire dissipated into a shower of dull sparks. The croak remaining in his throat after he stopped couldn't be mistaken.

"If there's anything you can do, I would greatly appreciate it. As things stand, I do not know if I will be able to Sing again."

He was being uncharacteristically emotional, but Garnas could not tell whether it was genuine or a ploy to garner sympathy.

"I might be able to do something," the woman said, in a very different tone.

Garnas wondered how much pull cantors actually had in the wider world. People kept treating Eilert as the leader.

She disappeared into a back room and stayed there just long enough for Garnas to grow bored, cross the marble tiled floor and sit on a hard wooden bench. Her smile was appreciably more genuine when she returned.

"I've been authorised to give you a carriage fee waiver for medical reasons. The fee was eight thalers per ticket, so your new total is fifty-seven thalers."

Eilert couldn't disguise his disappointment. He turned to the others.

"It was worth a try. I guess it's only a week until—"

"No."

Shirin stepped forwards.

"We agreed you need to get treated as soon as possible," she said. "It's not just the week waiting here, it's the extra week of journey time. We can afford two tickets. Use them for you and Garnas. If I can't rustle up another fourteen thalers by tomorrow morning, then I'll join you when I'm able to."

"I can hold the third ticket for you. It won't be sold before tomorrow," the assistant said, helpfully.

Eilert didn't appear happy at the idea of splitting their group up, but he could find no will to argue. He had to go, if anyone did, and it was hardly fair to leave Garnas alone when he knew no-one and had no money of his own. Defeated, he nodded.

"I'll prepare your travel documents. Your friend needs to be added to our system. If you could step into the next room, sir..."

The 'next room' had decor just as opulent as the main area, but in a smaller room it felt crowded and oppressive. Garnas placed himself on the only seat he could see. What he had taken to be an esoteric piece of sculpture blinked one outsized eye at him. A second glance confirmed that the 'eye' was a magnifying lens, behind which an ordinary-sized man sat cocooned by a delicate metal apparatus consisting mostly of jointed arms. The uniform helped him blend into the wall.

"Please look into the blue light and state your name clearly."

"Garnas." He felt self-conscious to have no family name or title.

Some of the arms jerked into new positions. More blue lights began to shine.

"And your point of origin?"

Seeing Garnas's uncertainty, the man explained.

"The world you were born into. It helps us keep our records clear, particularly when two people have a similar name."

"Oh. Um..."

Garnas felt reluctant to share it. Not out of any sense of shame, but because it seemed to do a disservice to the place he had spent most of his life to sum it up in the two words the sailors had used. But then, any place where people lived could be only *summarised* in words, at best. The feeling of a place—the truth of it—defied language.

"The rust graveyard."

On the other side of the lens, an eyebrow lifted. That gesture of surprise was the only emotion the man had shown so far.

He leaned around his machinery and passed a small card to Garnas. His name was printed across the top, followed by his 'point of origin', and then underneath was a metallic square, shimmering in the gaslights.

"Is this right?" the assistant prompted.

Garnas nodded.

The man took the card back and rubbed the metallic part with his thumb. When he gave it to Garnas a second time, there was a glowing shape above it. A likeness of Garnas's head, picked out in sharp blue spots. It turned slowly, independent of the card, then faded from sight. It was only his desire to avoid looking like a rube that kept Garnas from rubbing the square to see if he could bring it back.

"For tomorrow's journey, will you be travelling with any weapons?"

"Yes, my long gun."

"Is it kept in a secure box?"

Garnas picked up his gun case, and showed off its heavy hasp and lock.

"Splendid. For our records, could you tell me the calibre of the firearm?"

Garnas, at a loss for units, held up his hands, a palm's width apart.

"To beg your pardon, when I spoke of 'calibre' I was referring to the inner diameter of the bore of the weapon."

"That's what I was speaking of, too."

This time it was both eyebrows.

#

The price of the ticket included an overnight stay in the spartan but tasteful rooms of the Starpenny Line building. It was a natural place for them to leave their luggage while they went in search of an early lunch.

The crowds bothered Garnas. The novelty of them had faded and he could not replicate the practised ease with which the other two slipped through the press of bodies. Every elbow found his ribs, every shoulder clashed with his own. He was used to being able to pick subtleties out of the smell in the air—the direction of the wind and the likelihood of rain—but since he had come ashore all he could smell was people. Not a rank smell, but a *full* one. What had started as ubiquitous had become pervasive, and now risked becoming suffocating.

To his great relief, they broke out of the throng and onto the frontage of a low, white-tiled building. Bats wheeled high overhead. A silent waiter took them to a table on the terrace overlooking the harbour. Goods from a dozen worlds passed through those docks, and the local businesses took their due portion.

The dishes that arrived were artfully presented, and the misgivings Garnas had been nursing vanished at his first taste. He considered himself something of an expert on the preparation of fish, but he had never had access to the delicate fruits flavouring his meal. He would not have imagined a sweet flavour would go so well.

"What can we do to find the extra money?" he asked, between mouthfuls.

"Well, 'we' won't do anything," Shirin said. "The only ways to make that kind of money at such short notice are dangerous. Probably technically illegal. Enough people are so desperate for money that they'll take any risk, which means there's also no shortage of people planning on exploiting them. Steering clear of that mess requires finesse. Getting left to face the music when the gendarmes arrive is possibly the least worst outcome."

She sighed wearily.

"No offence, Garnas, but this isn't your forte. You don't know the area, you don't have the contacts. It isn't Eilert's, either. It's up to me."

From the tone of her voice it was clear she was accustomed to taking such risks, if not exactly with pleasure.

Garnas's eyes dropped to the axe Shirin always carried. It was good decorum to go unarmed in the streets of Grand Billon—work knives did not count—but weapons of cultural importance were tolerated provided they remained sheathed or otherwise out of harm's way. Shirin had put a cloth cover on the head of her axe and moved its carrying loop to the centre of her back. This was apparently sufficient for it to go unremarked.

Shirin saw him looking and misinterpreted his glance.

"I've never got involved in anything *really* bad before and I don't plan on it now. I just need to find someone looking for temporary muscle. Someone to look dangerous and dissuade troublemakers."

Garnas felt a knot of doubt in his stomach.

"That sort of job pays the kind of money we need?"

"Not usually. But an axe like mine has a certain cachet and demands a higher price. I might have to agree to do more work once we come back. That I can live with. It's the time frame that's the tricky part."

Eilert's fork skewered the last of his fish with an insouciance belying his concern.

"I would never forgive myself," he said, "if you made a bad decision on my account. If you can't find something harmless enough, we can wait for you at the cathedral. I'm going home, not into mare incognitum."

Shirin nodded. The scrape of her chair against the floor as she stood up was abrasive.

"I'll start looking. You two take in the sights."

#

Grand Billon was a trade town. Its veins ran with coin. There was scant room between the warehouses and the financial offices to accommodate the tourist trade, but anywhere that sat at the confluence of a hundred trading routes would accrue spectacles aplenty. Denizens of nearby worlds, separated from their homelands only by the interstice, had raised architecture in their own styles, punctuating the flat-roofed terraces or merging into them in unexpected ways.

The ships in the dock showed even more variety. Eilert pointed out the different sail configurations as they strolled past. Square rigging, junk rigging, rigging fore and aft—and those were just the vessels that used sails. A pair of trimarans bristled with oars. Eilert commented off-handedly that it was an odd combination, and Garnas knew so little he didn't even understand why. One particularly wide ship sat between paddle-wheels and the next one along was a squat metal box with rounded corners and no windows or doors to be seen—the *Star Risen*. She was to be tomorrow's transport.

Garnas felt abruptly melancholy. The presence of so many ships drove home how little he had travelled. All those miles had been walking through familiar territory. His eyes had never seen beyond the horizon, as others' had. A rush of frustration at needing to wait before he could be on the move again swept over him.

Perhaps Eilert could see some of his mood, because the cantor took them away from the docks now, into one of the many market squares crowded with stalls. A bored gendarme sat in a booth, surrounded by yellowing flyers offering rewards about lawbreakers known to the port authorities. A stern notice advised the curious that notes issued by foreign organisations would not be honoured.

"Let me know if you see anything interesting," Eilert said. "We can afford one or two treats without jeopardising the third ticket—"

He was talking to himself. Garnas had headed up some steps to one of the permanent businesses that overlooked the square. Eilert hurried after him, into a shop specialising in firearms and ammunition. The shopkeeper was a birdlike man, and the sparse plumage on his head spoke of advanced age.

"What interests you, friend?" he asked.

Garnas stood with hands pressed to the glass of a display case. Plush but aged velvet lined it, and spaced at intervals were large calibre cartridges. Each was presented with a copperplate card naming and describing it like a confectioner's tray of truffles—'armour piercing', 'expanding', 'marking round', 'needle and sabot'.

"Are these the largest calibre munitions you stock? I'm looking for—" Garnas rustled as he looked through his boarding papers "—fifteen-sixteenths bore shells suitable for use with compressed air propellant."

The shopkeeper came out from behind the counter. The plainness of his apron belied the colours of his feathers, although they looked to be just as sparse on his body as they were on his head. He was colourful by birth but beige by trade and choice. His pot belly made a bulge in the dark leather apron that resembled cannon shot.

"An exotic size, sure enough. Archaic, even."

He scratched his neck.

"It sounds like you might be sporting a museum piece. Are you sure you want to fire it at all?"

Garnas looked thoughtful.

"It's in service, but I guess it's based on an old design."

The birdman nodded enthusiastically.

"That makes sense. My friend, I think the weapon you have is measured differently to more modern pieces. Fifteen-sixteenths would, I suspect, be ever so slightly too wide."

"It would jam."

"Probably. As luck would have it I have the tools to custom-make shells to fit properly, even if I do not carry any in stock. It will take a day or two, though. How many were you thinking of?"

"None immediately, thank you. I have enough for now, but I may need to restock in future. I will definitely swing by here if I'm in Grand Billon when the need arises."

"As you say, my friend."

The shopkeeper stroked his chin. He climbed a short ladder to a high shelf behind him and fetched down a dusty wooden chest. From inside he produced a pair of shells, brass-cased and worn.

"Would you like to take these away to test if they are a good fit? They're technically antiques, built to the old size system."

Garnas accepted them happily.

"I would, yes. What time do you close today? I won't be able to return them tomorrow."

The shopkeeper waved away his question.

"Consider them a gift. They've been here for years without being sold. Do with them as you wish, my friend."

Garnas turned them over in his hands as they left the shop. Details of their type were stamped onto their bases. They were finer craftsmanship than the ones he made at home.

"You could probably get your ammunition from one of the workshops on the docks at half the price," Eilert said.

"I would prefer to deal with someone at least partially familiar with my gun. It's finicky."

"I see. Come on, there's something I want to show you. I think you'll appreciate it."

The climb to the top of the town was long. Garnas was well used to walking hunchbacked terrain, but he had to stop for Eilert to catch his breath. The higher they got, the more of Grand Billon they could see. Wharves, large and small, dominated the view. The *Shaved Link* was lost amongst them. Buildings in upper Grand Billon were mostly built from brown stone. The roofs were flat but followed the slope of the hill. Elaborately carved wooden shutters were closed against the afternoon sun over glassless windows. After the riot of colour and the mishmash of architectural styles below it almost seemed drab.

The brown of the roofs was what Garnas had taken to be a bare hillside when they had arrived. He had greatly underestimated the size of the town.

Eilert turned off the road and onto a plaza. Wide flagstones marked out a flat area with an uninterrupted view of the sea. Set into the ground, in seemingly random places, were three iron prongs. Each was somewhat shorter than the average person and ended in a blunt point. Garnas just had time to dwell on how they looked like accidents waiting to happen before Eilert gently pulled him over to the inland side of the square, where there was a small dais, with another

147

prong on it. This one had numbered gradations marked in it. Underneath was a stone plinth with calendar calculations that Eilert ran his fingers along while he did arithmetic under his breath.

"Okay, close one eye and line the other up with the third notch down from the top," he said.

Garnas did so.

"So, to your left you see the red marker? If you look at the sea right where the tip is, it should be mistier than normal. Can you make it out?"

Garnas couldn't at first. It was only when he scanned down from the horizon and found the mark that he could see where the sea was more blurred.

"That's the transition point we came in by. The other markers show the others. This is what makes Grand Billon such an important nexus: three transitions into different parts of the interstice. Some ships don't even bother stopping here. In one, out another."

When Garnas stepped away, he saw three other carved plinths, aligned with the spikes. Each listed the places one could reach by entering the interstice through that point. The names were all strange to him. Some were written using glyphs he didn't recognise. He read the first list several times without finding what he was looking for.

"The rust graveyard isn't mentioned," Eilert said. "Maybe whoever built this didn't know it existed."

Garnas felt abruptly rudderless. He only had to consult his memory to know how few people lived at his home, but it still seemed wrong that it went completely unremarked. It was everything he had ever known until a few weeks ago and it didn't even merit a mention.

Eilert tried to reassure him that the omission didn't matter, that every place was important to someone and that the missing name said more about the people who built the sculpture than Garnas's home, but he couldn't find the words. He knew how to weave words fancily, Shirin knew how to speak from the heart.

"Let's go back to the food market," he ended up saying. "I'm in the mood for some bao."

#

Bao bought and eaten, they returned to the Starpenny Line building. Shirin had left a note for them at the front desk. Fearful that it might contain details of less than salubrious activities, they waited until they were in their room before opening it.

'Job found. Expect to be back just after midnight.'

"Terse," Garnas said.

"Shirin always writes as though she resents the expenditure of ink," Eilert observed.

There was nothing in it about what they should do if she wasn't back in time.

Garnas had slept poorly on the *Shaved Link*. It wasn't just that he was unused to sailing, on the sea or through the interstice, but also that the excitement of travel had enervated him so. It was hard to keep his eyes open when he lay down.

It was dark when he woke. Eilert was propped up, reading a book by a gaslight turned down low.

"Sorry, I didn't mean to doze off."

"If you needed it, you needed it." Eilert smiled. "Did you sleep well?"

Garnas didn't get a chance to answer. Someone knocked politely on their door. Eilert set his book down and crossed the carpet barefoot. The crack of the open door revealed a short man thrusting an envelope.

"Urgent message," he said, brusquely, and snatched his hand away as soon as Eilert took it.

The door closed. Eilert tore the envelope open.

"I didn't even know they had porters here," Eilert muttered. "It would have saved me—"

Garnas sat up, wondering why Eilert had fallen silent. The cantor usually maintained an expression of affable detachment, but what he had read cut through to the core.

"It's a ransom demand for Shirin."

A thought that had been clamouring for Garnas's attention finally broke through.

"He wasn't in uniform."

Eilert threw the door open again. The slump in his shoulders made it clear the 'porter' was long gone. Eilert was not the hunter Garnas was, though. Whereas Eilert had thought to chase, Garnas's instinct was to lie in wait where he knew the prey would pass. In this case, the alley underneath their window.

The streets in this part of Grand Billon were quiet in the evening. Starpenny Line had planted its headquarters well away from the cafés and inns that kept their doors open throughout the night. There was only one man hurrying past, and there could be no mistaking his clothes.

It was only a one-storey drop, but Garnas landed hard enough to splay the man on the cobbles like a bearskin. His swearing swiftly turned into tight groans as a cracked rib shifted.

"I do not have time for nonsense," Garnas whispered in his ear. "You will tell me where she is being held, by whom, how many of them there are, and how they are armed."

The man kept silent until Garnas brought his skinning knife right up to his face. Light from distant lamps reflected off a worn handle and a frequently-sharpened blade. A knife wasn't seen as a weapon, not until it was used as one.

"The south docks. White cross warehouse. Fellkar heard there was a bounty on her. Figured we could collect more from you."

"How many? Weapons?" Garnas kept his voice patient, like he was speaking to a child.

"Four. But Fellkar's worth ten men. Swords. Bows."

Garnas drew his knife back slightly, but didn't sheathe it.

"Now your boots."

"What?"

"I can't have you getting there before me. So, boots."

The man's hands were shaking as he removed them. Garnas pulled the laces out and tied his hands behind him. He threw the boots over a wall and left. It would not take long for the man to free himself, but it would be long enough.

As he strode out of the alleyway Eilert emerged from the building.

"I'm fetching my gun. We're going to get Shirin back."

"We don't have anything like the ransom—" Eilert began.

"I don't plan on making a trade. I know where she's being held. You can get us there, I hope?"

Eilert spoke carefully. He hadn't seen that lance-like focus in Garnas since the stormy night on top of the factory.

"I don't think she'd want us to do that."

"I know," Garnas said quietly. He almost told Eilert about the bounty, but something warned him he'd want to take the words back if he did. "Whatever trouble she's found, she knew it was a possibility. If we miss our ship it would have all been for nothing. But if I wasn't here, the two of you would be upstairs waiting for your departure time."

"If you weren't here, we wouldn't be either."

Garnas nodded to concede that point. Eilert pressed on.

"It's just the two of us."

"One of us is a cantor. Apparently that means something around here."

"I can't Sing."

"They don't know that." Garnas paused in the doorway, then added: "Some things you just have to do, you know?"

#

Darkness meant little at the main docks. Ships came and went at all hours and they needed their cargo handling. There was always bustle directly waterside but sometimes goods needed to be stored while awaiting their assigned vessel. This created the need for premises further inland. Such warehouses were little more than brick boxes with wide doors, usually kept shut tight with chains. Their owners, businessmen to a fault, saw an empty warehouse as lost money and were not above renting them out to anyone who passed a consideration their way, provided they could pretend to the authorities and their own consciences that nothing illicit was taking place.

Finding the warehouse was easy. It was the only one nearby with light inside and with its doors left slightly ajar. Nothing so suspicious as to draw attention, but a sign to those in the know that they should keep their heads down as they passed.

One person was standing outside the warehouse when Garnas and Eilert arrived. The man's studied air of casualness would have convinced no-one, and it evaporated when he saw them.

"I know you weren't expecting to see us until tomorrow," Eilert said, holding up his hands to show he was unarmed. "But we have a schedule. We can get this done now."

"No tricks?"

Eilert kept his empty hands showing, as if to emphasise that they had come alone, long before the gendarmes could have possibly organised a raid. The guard's eyes narrowed when he saw the long gun hanging from its strap at Garnas's back.

"You go armed?"

"I just want to make sure no-one does anything rash," Garnas said as nonchalantly as he could. "I'm not the threat here."

He left it deliberately unclear as to whether he meant that the real threat was the kidnappers, or Eilert's magic.

"Wait," the guard said, and slid through the doors.

The lack of windows meant they didn't have to fear getting shot at through them. It was tense enough anyway.

"Inside." The man pushed the door slightly wider and beckoned them.

The interior was lit by a single lamp at the far end. Shadows black and steepled danced on the walls and high roof. When the door closed behind them even such a large space felt suffocating.

Shirin had rope coiled around her middle, pinioning her arms, and she sported the beginnings of an impressive black eye, but she looked otherwise unharmed. The lookout stayed behind Garnas and Eilert, the better to intimidate. Two men in leather armour had arrows nocked and aimed at the newcomers. Between them stood the lioness woman that they has seen earlier on the docks. Tall, proud and completely in control of the situation. Fellkar, evidently.

Eilert held Garnas's lock-box high, in a pretence that it held the ransom money.

"Put it on the floor," Fellkar said.

Eilert didn't do so.

"Not with taut bowstrings."

Fellkar waved an arm, and the archers lowered their weapons.

"Now proof of life. Are you still with us, Shirin?"

"We're going to discuss this later," her voice was hoarse, "but yes."

Eilert made a great show of placing the box on the floor and working the lock. He paused just a moment before flipping it open and reaching inside. Fellkar and the archers could only see the lid, and the lookout could only see Eilert's back. In silence, a single faint note rang out, the gentle whistle of the long gun building pressure. The kidnappers didn't—couldn't—know what it meant.

Holding down the trigger behind his back had been awkward, but Garnas had loosened the strap to make it easier. When he pulled the weapon in front of him he had only a moment to take aim, but the practice of years made it almost easy.

"I'm sorry," he said, and shot Shirin in the stomach.

A wet explosion of red spattered over the floor, and the *boom* of the weapon's report echoed back from the walls. Bows were drawn ready to fire but in that instant Garnas had his hands in the air in surrender.

"There's no point," Eilert said quickly. "We didn't have the money but we couldn't let you take her. If you want more dead bodies..." he drew breath as if he was about to Sing.

Fellkar barked out a short laugh.

"I like your style," she said. "If you can't win, force a draw? But a costly draw for you."

"It's how my people do things," Garnas shrugged. "Are you planning to still be here when the gendarmes arrive?"

Fellkar wasted no breath replying to the question, but stood back.

"What's left of her is all yours." She gestured to Shirin's body. "Move away from the doors."

The two parties engaged in a distrustful shuffling dance until Fellkar's crew slipped out of the door and into the night.

As Garnas and Eilert knelt over Shirin, she started to cough.

"What did you do to me?" she spluttered.

"Marking round," Garnas said. "Basically a can of paint with a fragile lid, courtesy of a generous shopkeeper. Eilert's idea to use it this way, though."

"Hurts like hell."

"I didn't have time to lower the chamber's pressure. Do you want to have that discussion you mentioned now, or tomorrow on the ship?"

Shirin might have been dazed but she still picked up on the important fact.

"Where did you get the money?"

"Guess who has a bounty on her head?" Garnas asked. Without waiting for an answer he continued: "Our friend Fellkar. 'A reward for information regarding the whereabouts of'. The gendarmes will have heard the shot. As soon as they arrive we can ask for the reward. I'll tell them we'll accept less if we can have it before tomorrow morning. It'll be enough for your ticket."

She smiled weakly.

Garnas couldn't smile back. He'd seen how she tensed when he said the word 'bounty'. She knew there was one on her own head. Fellkar apparently hadn't wanted to risk trying to collect it, not with her own to worry about, and had opted to demand ransom instead. That hesitancy was what had made Garnas suspicious, and he had passed a gendarmes' office on the way to the docks where he confirmed his hunch.

"A discussion tomorrow, then," Shirin conceded.

She hesitated, as if she was about to say something else, but did not. Garnas knew she must have her reasons to keep her secrets, but he trusted her enough to let things lie.

For now.

BEN WRIGHT

Caelum Cathedrale

I'm not afraid of heights. Who could be, here?

The cistern looked smaller than I remembered it. A seventeen-hundred pace circumference wasn't as imposing as it used to be, when it constituted most of my world. The wayliner *Star Risen* lay tied up at the docks. I don't really care for those nasty, boxy things, to be honest. They are comfortable, reliable and by lor' are they *fast*, but spending the voyage in a windowless, individual cabin robs travel of a certain romance.

On this occasion I had cherished solitude, I'll admit. I'd been putting on a brave face for the others for long enough. A chance to relieve pressure—pressure I wasn't fully aware even existed—had been welcome. The downside was it had left me alone with my thoughts. I'm not normally one to mope, but I had been acutely aware that every breve that passed took me closer to a discussion I was terrified to have, a discussion likely to end with gently-broken but horrifying disappointment.

As we stepped off the wood of the docks and onto the stone of the Cathedral Tower, I watched Garnas. In most ways he's a practical and competent fellow. Please understand that what I mean is that he had already, in the short time I'd known him, demonstrated an unshowy type of heroism in saving lives, my own included. But in moments like this, when he was confronted with something new and strange and far outside his previous experience, he took on an aspect of childlike wonder it was impossible not to be charmed by.

And what was he looking at? The Cathedral towers, reaching into the sky around the cistern. Four of them were at the corners, the "old towers" we call them. Their conical roofs were added latterly and in a hurry, and did not quite match the quality of the older stonework. The Remembrance Tower, still technically under construction on one side of the square, was not yet quite as tall but was much wider. The focal point for the life of the Cathedral, full of pomp.

The sky was the same blue it always was: the blue of my jacket and the blue of the pennants hanging from the towers. In the mid-afternoon sun the pale stone almost looked silver. It's the scene I think of whenever I remember my adoptive home, and I was pleased it was at its best for Garnas's first look.

What makes that vista so striking is, of course, not so much what it contains as what it lacks. It's subtle at first. Shirin knew what I was thinking, I'm sure, because she helped steer Garnas away from the cistern and towards the edge. In the shadow of the north-west tower the air was cooler and one noticed the wind. The railings bore a new layer of lacquer from my remembered version of them. I mourned the old, worn look.

At the edge of the building, Garnas placed his hands on them and stared. I watched his knuckles turn white.

"How—how far down does it go?" he asked in a small voice.

"Ah," I responded. "One of the deep, philosophical questions. It goes down as far as anyone has cared to check. Below there, what does it matter?"

"The tower has to stand on something," he objected.

I shrugged. Some things just Were, and confounded any attempt to probe at 'why?'.

"The weight," he added. "The wind. Something has to keep it from collapsing."

I winked at Shirin and she rolled her eyes. Officially, I was not permitted to reveal any of the secrets of the Chorus, but if Garnas was already thinking in those terms he would probably work it out himself before long.

"The clouds down there are poisonous, *and* corrosive. Every now and then someone comes along with the bright idea of lowering themselves in a bathyscaphe. Some of them even make it back up to safety. You can't see anything in that soup, so they learn nothing either way."

As if to underscore my point, the roiling orange mass was briefly lit by lightning, flowering somewhere deep and hostile. It was scores of levels down from us, distant and toy-like. The clouds' colour gradually changed to match the sky the closer to horizontal you looked.

Shirin looked a little impatient; probably an affectation. She was not immune to scenes of grandeur. Hard to appreciate them once you know the Cathedral better, though. I'm ashamed it took me so long. Garnas hadn't had the shine taken off yet. I wanted to let him enjoy it.

It's the only place outside the interstice with no horizon.

#

Guest accommodation is in the north-west tower, and it has never been private rooms. I'd seen nothing unusual about cramped dormitories until I'd been travelling long enough to realise how rare such an arrangement was. I scarcely needed to warn the two of them to keep their valuables on them at all times. The proctors would not waste their time on the petty crimes of outsiders, whether perpetrators or victims, and there was little I could do to help. Well, that's not strictly true; a word here or there might goad the proctors out of indifference, but I needed to use all the political pull I could muster elsewhere.

I wasn't ready.

The lie I told myself was that I was laying the groundwork for what I needed to do, but it rang hollow, even to me. The plain fact was that I was scared.

No cantor is entirely without allies in the Cathedral. I went in search of one.

The south-west tower is largely set aside for the instruction of novitiates. The chambers too small to see use as practice rooms are mostly storage, but the attic space, being acoustically dire, had been reserved as a rather fine apartment. Unless things had changed greatly in my absence—which, this being the Cathedral, was never the case—there was only one person senior enough to warrant such spacious accommodation but who tolerated the proximity to the lowest orders.

As luck would have it, she was available.

"Thank you for seeing me at such short notice, Maestra Baritone."

The clink of a decanter, handled carelessly in haste, was my only answer at first.

"I have had an entire day of 'Maestra this' and 'Maestra that'," she grumbled. "I am tired and I only let you in because I was too surprised to see you to say 'no'. Let me be Dieuwke to you today."

She slid sideways onto an ottoman and toasted my impertinence. No refreshment was offered to me. I think she wanted to see if I was bold enough to help myself. She had a few more wrinkles than I remembered, and maybe she moved a little more slowly, but scant else had changed.

"But as you're already here, Eilert, we might as well talk. Goodness knows you didn't deign to grace your old teacher with your presence to let me know you were leaving. I assume your return must herald something grave."

She had the same air of acerbic grumpiness, the one that had nearly led me to some very foolish actions as a confused youth still finding his way in the world. In all honesty, if she'd shown the least interest in me I would have succumbed to her charms in an instant, propriety be damned.

Most people's sexuality has an exception, and she was mine.

It was difficult to tell how much of her persona was an act. Maybe even she didn't know. The one thing she couldn't hide was the strain. As the only member of the council who wasn't in it purely for personal power, she had to spend a lot of time watching bad decisions be made in spite of her. It showed in her face. In how the whisky glass trembled in her hand.

She steered the conversation towards small talk. Every time I tried to bring up why I was there, the treatment I sought, she found a way to divert me. It took me a while to realise why. I have no aptitude for politics.

She already knew. Contacts in the Starpenny Line company, perhaps. Dancing about the issue allowed her to continue to pretend that she *didn't* know. Apparently it was politically inexpedient for her to be known to know. My story trailed off somewhere in the jungle while I tried to work out why.

Despite her professed tiredness, she had crossed to the far wall and traced the outline of a stone with a finger while we talked. It was at a place where repairs were visible, the smaller and rougher stones mortared to the grand original stones. The repairs had been made in a hurry, long before my time, which was why they were lower quality. Dieuwke seldom did anything without purpose. Was she counselling caution, or haste?

The older masonry bears a frieze that predates any Cathedral records. The official interpretation is that it explains the folly of 'folk singing', as opposed to the formal Song of the Cathedral's teachings. We Sing *along* with the world around us, picking up harmonies already there and creating new resonance, whereas hedge singers merely sing *across* the world, which is why their songs have no power. "Their every bar rubato and their every interval a comma", the aphorism goes. There was a time when I believed it fully. Why was she drawing my attention to it?

When I realised I had fallen silent I dragged my attention back to my story, but this time I took care to tiptoe around any mention of Singing. I confined myself to the adventure.

"This new friend of yours," Dieuwke interrupted, returning to her ottoman. "Is he novice material?"

My words trailed off. Garnas's voice had none of the special harmonics my ears were trained to hear. He was as deaf to the subtle voice of the world as most people were. I hadn't even thought about him in relation to my official mission. Of course—I'd been too worried about my immediate problem to see the difficulty. Those of us who left the Cathedral did so to find new voices, bright young novices to train. For many it was a sacred calling. For the rest of us, it was a convenient pretext to get away from the oppressive Cathedral and all of its pettiness and cruelty. I had been gone for a considerable time, returned empty-handed, and then only to ask for a boon. Leaving in the first place had cost me what markers I had.

She had asked her question to make me remember all that.

#

Part of me wanted my friends to be there when I put my case to the council, but the balance of me would not have been able to bear it if they had borne witness to my humiliation. It had seemed such a simple prospect when we first made plans to return to the Cathedral. It was in the council's power to withhold care that might restore my voice and, Dieuwke aside, it was not in their nature to do anyone a favour without something in return.

I would not be pleading my case before anything as formal as a tribunal. Formality would imply a certain degree of even-handedness. The collegiate atmosphere of the meeting belied the fact that, should it not go well, matters could take a very grim turn for me.

The Remembrance Tower eschewed the use of bare stone for its walls. Wooden panelling was everywhere, every piece of which would have been imported at great expense. The old towers had an effortless majesty that the gaudiness of the new one could only aspire to. The Cathedral was rich, or at least, vast quantities of money flowed in and out of it with regularity. Truth be told, if it could not sell the services of its cantors so dearly then it would not be able to feed itself. The wayliner we arrived in had been half filled with food. The machinations of the council are not entirely due to personal greed, despite what the cynic in me says. They have to be just as rapacious in their dealings with the outside world.

I knocked.

"Enter."

I tried to smile as I walked in. In lieu of a greeting I made brief eye contact with each of the council in turn.

Fulmorn, Maestro Bass, pretended not to notice me as I entered. He had three of his students with him, favoured not for their aptitude with their voice but for their eagerness to share his bed. I did my best to keep my distaste hidden.

Katka, Maestra Soprano, with the face of an angel. It belied her proclivities behind closed doors. She took a special interest in her most talented students, and when they became full cantors they were, without exception, brilliant, disciplined and irreparably broken.

Dieuwke nodded at me. Before she had started drinking in earnest her unusually deep voice had been the most powerful the Cathedral had seen in generations. She had never quite returned to her full strength even after getting her consumption under control.

Athol, Maestro Alto. His thin, expressionless face said that if he had any vices, they were so rarefied as to be almost unrecognisable as such. He had propelled himself into becoming the undisputed first among equals in his twentieth year, and was still going strong a century later. I knew to fear him above all else.

"You understand we are all very busy," Athol said, gesturing for me to take a seat. "We need to keep this brief."

My heart sank at his words. This was exactly how a swift refusal would go. Except, I realised, there would have been no purpose in summoning me were that the case. A simple message would have sufficed.

Katka leaned forwards.

"The resources of our hospital have been stretched thin lately. Too many choirs have suffered casualties. For a time we were convinced some enemy of the Cathedral was orchestrating a campaign against us sub rosa. We had to expend a number of agents to establish that it really was simply poor luck."

I did not ask how the agents had been 'expended'.

"However, we are of a mind to prioritise your case," Athol continued for her, "at the insistence of your mentor. All the reports we have received about you indicate you have been a credit to the reputation of the Cathedral, even in challenging circumstances. This is something we value particularly highly, given the recent difficulties."

Joy and trepidation fought for my heart. I was going to be fixed, presumably at some terrible price.

"Your recovery will likely take a week or two," Athol continued, "and I understand that it will be a few days before treatment can begin. We can hardly interrupt courses of treatment already in progress."

"We have a job for you while you wait," Fulmorn interrupted.

In the silence that followed, Athol turned away from me for the first time and stared at the other Maestro. Fulmorn pretended to be preoccupied with getting his wine refilled by one of his hangers-on to cover his discomfort.

"As my astute colleague implies, our shortage of personnel has left us with an excess of tasks as compared to available cantors," Athol returned his gaze to me. "Since you are here, and you aren't occupied with the induction of any new pupils, all we ask is for you to not be idle while you wait for the ministrations of the cantors medica."

Dieuwke reached for a glass that wasn't there; a reflexive gesture.

"This is a matter of some delicacy," she added, "so we can't trust it to someone who hasn't achieved cantor. It also carries a degree of risk."

Reading between the lines, the council had probably intended to 'volunteer' someone from her chorus before I arrived. If the task was dangerous, better have it fall to one of Dieuwke's ill-behaved whelps than someone who mattered. My arrival had given her an opportunity to punt it away again. The rest of the council believed it was getting one over on her this way, forcing her to choose between a former student and a current one; when in fact this outcome was exactly what she wanted. I don't know if it spoke of her confidence in me, or her willingness to hang me out to dry.

"I understand," I said, for her benefit more than the others. "Is this a good time to discuss the nature of this task?"

Fulmorn swallowed his drink quickly.

165

"The subcistern reaches are not of interest to us the majority of the time," he said, giving the word 'subcistern' an edge I had almost forgotten in my time away. "However. It has come to our attention that someone is Singing down there."

The area beneath the Cathedral proper is essentially a slum, albeit displaced vertically rather than horizontally. It's considered parasitic by the Cathedral. Apart from the people born there, it has a steady influx of new arrivals—travellers who have absconded from their vessel and students from the Cathedral who prove unable to master their potential. The ability to Sing is a rare gift, rare enough for cantors to need to travel widely to find anyone with even a hint of it. Conventional wisdom held that no-one from the subcistern levels would ever prove capable of it.

"The voice is faint but persistent," Maestra Katka said. "Naturally, it needed to be investigated. I sent Cantor Cayha. She has not returned, and the aberrant Singing continues."

Someone from Katka's chorus would not have hesitated to silence the voice, with violence if necessary. I began to like this task less and less.

"You are allowed to take whoever you want with you when you investigate," Dieuwke said.

Her use of 'allowed' implied that while I could ask anyone, I could command no-one. I saw the trap. If I failed because no other cantor was prepared to risk their own neck, it would be judged as my personal failure and taken as grounds to withhold my treatment.

I caught Maestro Athol's gaze and he held eye contact for an unsettlingly long time.

"This matter is of utmost importance," he said, unusually quietly. "We have concerns that this new voice might, deliberately or by accident, interfere with the Eternal Round."

There was the hook. Until then I had had half a mind to abandon them to their politics and their injured pride. 'Concern', nothing—they were terrified. If the Eternal Round was interrupted it would spell death not just for everyone in the Cathedral, but everyone in the regions below it. The interloper hadn't caused a catastrophe yet, but desperation might drive them to it if the cantors of the Cathedral descended into the depths in full force. Sending an outsider was an advantage, if any cantor could really be considered an outsider.

I had no choice but to acquiesce.

#

My medical consultation was brief, even for a preliminary one. If the doctor had any suspicion that I would fail to return, he kept it well hidden. I was under the strictest of instructions to avoid any attempt to Sing until further notice.

I was never sure if the council had expected me to take Shirin and Garnas with me, but frankly I had little alternative. It wasn't as if I would have been able to stop either of them once they knew I was heading into danger. A cantor's skill hadn't been enough to protect Cayha, so my inability to Sing was not an issue. Both of my friends had talents alien to the Cathedral and its vast undercroft. I hoped they might prevail where magic had failed.

I told them as much as I could. They needed to be aware of the danger. Some details would not make sense to them, ones involving secrets of the Cathedral I was forbidden to share. More accurately, I could not share them where I might be overheard. It was dispiriting how swiftly I had readjusted to the paranoia of my 'home'. It only made me more confident of my decision to leave. Now if only I could manage the trick a second time...

The cistern was deeper than people guessed. The space between it and the outer walls was where the mundane business of the Cathedral took place—laundries, larders and so on. I could almost pretend I was giving a guided tour.

The fields were the most impressive. Mirrors fanned out around the tower, throwing light into an interior otherwise doomed to remain dark. Secondary mirrors reflected the light downwards. I chose a scenic route through decorative gardens. I said I wanted the two of them to see the Cathedral at its best but I was actually procrastinating.

There were fewer vegetables than I remembered. Some of those fields had been replanted with flowers and the beginning of a series of pergolas. It would be years before they achieved their full potential. In hindsight, it's obvious that the gardens had all been fields once. Maybe they'd even been able to feed the entire population. As wealth came in, those humble rows had been remade into something more befitting of the Cathedral's opulence. I hoped it would not turn out to be a mistake.

"The light is wrong," Garnas said, "but it makes everything mysterious."

"Whenever I felt overwhelmed by my studies I used to come here to unwind. I credit this rose garden in particular with all of my successes."

"That explains why it's so limp and disappointing," Shirin was uncharacteristically acerbic. Something had left her on edge since we had disembarked from the *Shaved Link*, and it emerged when she was tense.

"There's something really special, if you follow me. Only a handful of us know about it."

Water for the gardens came directly from the cistern, through copper pipes to spigots in alcoves in the walls. At some point the layout of one garden had changed. If you squeezed behind a hedge you could find your way into an alcove where all the pipework had been removed.

"Now what?" Garnas asked.

I shushed him and waited. Sure enough we could just hear some distant voices, brought to us through the channel that used to contain the pipe.

"Is that your, you know, special kind of singing?" Garnas asked.

I'd seen no-one else on this level. We probably had as much secrecy here as we would ever get.

"Not everyone who learns how to Sing becomes a cantor," I said. "Only about a third of us manage it. What you're hearing is a choir made up of people in the other two-thirds. They meet in hidden rooms throughout the Cathedral for this recital."

Shirin was paying close attention. When we'd first met I hadn't been ready to talk about the Cathedral. Once I'd loosened up a little it hadn't seemed relevant.

"What does this song do?" she asked.

I needed to work up to it.

"They're in the middle of a four and a half hour piece. Once they finish, they get a three and a half hour break before they Sing a reprise. Then they sleep for ten hours before they get up to do it all again tomorrow."

"Doesn't sound like much of a life," Garnas muttered.

I shrugged. It wasn't a fulfilling life, but better than many.

"There are two other shifts, meeting in different rooms, offset by eight hours in either direction. But that still leaves gaps, so there's another set of three shifts offset by four hours. The entire system is in place so at least two choirs are Singing at any given time. Even if something goes wrong, there will always be one choir Singing."

169

Describing the baroque protocol had made it clear how important it was.

"We call it the Eternal Round. If it ever stopped, the Cathedral would collapse."

Shirin looked thoughtful. Garnas started to laugh, but stopped short when he saw I was serious.

"We nearly lost the tower once," I said quietly.

The choristers in the Eternal Round didn't even know. It was knowledge for cantors only. Once I had been told, the clues in the architecture were obvious. The cistern wasn't originally the top of the tower, but a few dozen floors down. What were now called the four old towers had been glorified staircases to the levels above it. Everything higher had fallen during the calamity, over seven hundred years ago.

The truth had given me nightmares. I dreamt of the floor falling away from me, slipping sideways, as the walls cracked and parted. The faces of my friends, as panicked as I was, all of us helpless to arrest our fall. Horrible sounds as entire rooms collapsed inwards. Screams. I grabbed at a banister, for all the good it did. I turned my head upwards, hoping that some miracle could save us, but there was no time for anyone to conjure up a Song. A strange moment of relief when I saw my room-mate on the cistern level, safe, abruptly shattered when a chunk of masonry slammed into him from above. When we had no more breath to scream, the sound of the wind in our ears made us deaf, anyway. We dropped into the mist, the fractured pieces of tower clearing a way before us. Further we plunged, sinking a well into the orange clouds. We fell for so long that the mist rolled back over the top of the clear area, taking away the sun. No Songs could save us now. All we had left to us was the sick dread, the uncertainty of how we would die. Would we hit a solid obstacle, or would we keep falling for so long that the clouds rolled over us to choke us and bubble our flesh? Maybe it would be kinder to Sing our own codas.

"Are you okay?" Shirin brought me back to myself.

"Yes, sorry," I hadn't thought about those nightmares in years. "I had a bit of a moment."

If the survivors knew what had interrupted the Eternal Round back then, they had taken the secret to their graves.

"This is why the council is so exercised by the voice they've heard," I paused. "If we lose the Eternal Round, there'd be no coming back. Even losing just the cistern would cut us off from the interstice."

"This strange voice hasn't interfered so far?" Shirin asked.

I shook my head.

"But if they're a prodigal talent, without proper training, they might do so by accident."

The silence stretched out. The alcove became claustrophobic and I turned to leave.

"I knew there had to be something," Garnas blurted out. "The tower was made by the cantors, wasn't it?"

We don't know. We *can't* know. The Cathedral records—all of them—were lost with the top of the tower. In truth, for all our posturing about ancient magic and timeless wisdom, what we had was stitched together from fragments. Even the council itself had originally been temporary. Maybe there had even been a Song to restore the tower, lost forever.

The Cathedral, as an organisation, might have been a miasma of politics and cruelty, but the people in it were worth saving.

#

I had always imagined there to be a sharp division between the lower levels of the Cathedral and the subcistern reaches. From the way it had been talked about, by my peers and by my teachers, the distinction was clear. The reality was different. The blue and grey attire of cantors grew rarer as we descended, and the paler blue of novitiates predominated. When we reached the workshops, artisans in dark grey made running repairs to furniture brought from above. By the time we reached the lowest Cathedral floors of all, where the night soil was left to mature into fertiliser, I was confronted with other colours. I even recognised some of the styles from places across the interstice.

I was shocked, then I was shocked that I had *been* shocked. I should have realised that the pressures to keep people down below were more subtle than bars and gates. That wouldn't have been the Cathedral's style. I'd come to terms with how sheltered I had been from the wider world growing up in the Cathedral, but now it was brought home to me how sheltered it had kept me even from itself.

How many floors could these people climb before a proctor politely but firmly advised them to go back where they belonged?

"Where do we go from here?" Shirin said.

"Down," I said.

I was not yet too conspicuous, but I would become so. After some thought I had decided against changing clothes. Cantor blue might mark me as an anomaly, but it also marked me as someone with powerful friends. I hoped it would be enough to ward away anyone who might want to take advantage of strangers.

"I'll see if I can hear the voice when we're somewhere less crowded," I added. "My listening skills don't match the council's."

"What do you intend to do when you find them?" Garnas shifted uneasily from foot to foot. I don't think he knew me well enough to understand how I abhorred the instigation of violence.

"We ask them to stop. Or, perhaps, Sing more quietly."

"And if they refuse?"

"We time our arrival at the cistern to be just before the wayliner leaves, run up the gangplank and never look back."

Instead of sleeping overnight I'd been lying awake thinking about the possibility. If I abandoned the mission, I abandoned my voice, but if the alternative was violence the decision came as easily as breathing. Even then the prospect of it had kept me awake all night.

Shirin knew I wasn't being flippant with my reply. Her confidence in my morals reassured me. Coming back to the Cathedral, and seeing it through older, wiser eyes, had radically changed how I thought about both it and about myself.

After two more flights of stairs the last vestiges of Cathedral influence slipped away. Were it not for the close roof and the endless sky visible through the slit windows it could easily have been any town we had passed through on our travels. Perhaps it wasn't so strange that I felt more at ease there than I had since the liner heaved to.

Everyone had masks. Some were simple cloth, others were leather cones with metal housings for heavy filters. It couldn't only be for fashion. I began to feel unprepared.

Garnas nudged me and discreetly pointed upwards. Bolted to the ceiling of this level was a set of huge fans. The metal blades whirred deceptively slowly. It was only when you adjusted your sense of scale that you realised how fast their edges were going. Sure enough, I felt a gentle but constant breeze blowing down on us. Garnas was more at home with machinery than me. Their purpose was obvious to him.

"They create positive air pressure in the lower levels. So less mist seeps in. It can only do so much, though, so people also have masks. The better the mask, the deeper you can go."

The parts of the tower I knew stood a considerable distance proud of the mist layer. If there was a need to go that far down regularly, there was a lot more to the subcistern than we in the Cathedral knew. Although... the council and their assistants were probably aware. The rest of us didn't need to know.

At least there was no possibility of us losing our way. Down was down.

It had been a few minutes since I had seen any novitiates. Our little group was attracting curious glances. Better to keep moving.

Shirin had unconsciously taken the lead. Whether it was because she felt that I, in my reduced state, needed protection, or because it helped conceal my blue robes I couldn't tell. When we turned out of a passageway to a grand staircase she stopped so suddenly I bumped into her and nearly sent her tumbling down the steps.

She gasped. It wasn't at my clumsiness.

The part of the tower we were entering was hollow. Empty space from one wall to the other, save for a central pillar. I knew the tower to be eight hundred paces to a side, and it was no narrower here. The space looked purely structural, unlike the dense corridors and rooms we had just left. And the height! I could see the bottom, I thought, but it bore a telltale orange tint. Here, then, was where the tower's builders—whoever they had been—had intended the liveable floors to end.

They had reckoned without human need and ingenuity. Into this void, people had come with ropes and planks and pitons, building their own platforms and walkways. Steel hawsers anchored the largest. Houses had been built, some straight onto the stone wall with only a ladder for access. Pulleys squeaked as lifting platforms, carrying both people and cargo, were hauled up and down by muscle power alone. There was more life here than there was above. The Cathedral was the true parasite.

We couldn't stay still for too long without disrupting foot traffic, so we let the crowd carry us down the steps. I had expected the platform to feel insecure, to have some spring under our feet, but it felt solid. With no other destination in mind, we ended up at the edge of it, where a reassuringly sturdy safety rail stopped people falling over the edge.

Remember I said I wasn't afraid of heights? I was a liar. Most heights don't bother me, but the long, vertical tunnel that rolled away from us there made my stomach heave.

"Let's not dawdle," Shirin said.

Gawping like tourists would not serve us well. Once we reached the bottom of the chamber I hoped the gulf would be more bearable. Maybe it would, as long as we remembered not to look up.

Garnas pointed to where a paternoster ran an eternal loop. It didn't reach anywhere near the bottom, but it was a start.

"See a few levels down?" I said. "A shop. It's selling masks. I think we're going to need some."

I hoped they wouldn't try to gouge us on price more than our pockets could handle.

It was impossible to get a paternoster car to ourselves. I counted eleven heads, including the child, packed into our car. As we stepped off, somewhat hurried for fear of missing our floor, I saw a collection box asking for donations towards its maintenance. It was best not to dwell on what might happen if the denizens of this place were insufficiently generous.

To my great relief, three masks worked out cheaper than I expected. Not the best kind of filters, but more substantial than the cloth ones. They didn't have to last.

There were only three other people sharing our paternoster car this time. I could let my breath out and relax a little. As I did so I felt the point of the knife in my back. From the way the others had frozen, they had felt the same.

"There's no need for this to get nasty," a voice said in my ear. In the circumstances I had expected an ugly voice, maybe one with a rasp or given to unpleasant chuckles, but this voice was light, almost conversational. Somehow that was worse. "We mind our business down here. You mind yours up there. We don't trespass and neither should you."

I cleared my throat but was cut off before I could say anything.

"To sing is to die."

I closed my mouth.

"When two of your kind come down here in as many weeks, people start to ask questions. Questions like 'Why didn't the first one come back from down below?', and 'What are you lot planning?'. And the people asking those questions want answers."

A gentle push on the shoulder told me this was our floor, whether we wanted it to be or not. We had been the recipients of curious looks before; now everyone pretended not to see us. There would be no help forthcoming. Whoever controlled these toughs wanted information, which meant they probably wouldn't kill us out of hand, but there were no guarantees as to what would happen if they didn't like our answers.

I heard whistling.

BEN WRIGHT

Subcistern

I thought at first it might have been coincidence. But when I listened again, the whistling came in the same pattern.

'Open berth to port; three ship lengths in'

We weren't at sea—hard to be less so—but the sailors' whistle code was unmistakable. Our lead captor was talking but my attention was elsewhere.

Then I saw.

One of the rickety lifts was descending, laden with cargo but also laden with the whistler, hidden somewhere amongst the boxes. The message repeated.

Neither Shirin nor Garnas knew the whistle code. I stealthily grabbed a hand from each of them. They both flinched, in more-or-less identical ways, which I would have found adorable and amusing in equal measure another time. I picked my moment, gathered my courage, and broke into a sprint. Our assailants were caught by surprise and we established a decent lead.

The chase would have been over swiftly if I didn't have a destination in mind, the path to which was unclogged by people. There was only a waist-high railing for us to negotiate, with a short jump onto the moving platform as it descended.

The three of us landed together and sent the platform swinging alarmingly. If we hadn't been able to grasp the ropes to steady ourselves, we would surely have been tipped off entirely. It swung like a pendulum and, somehow, avoided being dashed against anything. We rode out the bumps in desperate silence.

Our saviour was a youth in practical brown garb. They had one of the more elaborate masks, complete with goggles, hung around their neck and ready to pull into place at a moment's notice. Our erstwhile captors were peering over the edge of the platform, visibly cursing. I hoped they weren't ruthless enough to try cutting the ropes.

"Heading upwards would be better," our rescuer said. "Harder for them to follow or interfere. Basically, your mistake was coming in from the top."

The sardonic twinkle in their eye told me it was not an entirely serious comment. I decided to trust them. What alternative did we have?

"I suspected that gentlefolk of travel such as yourselves would know the whistles. Even if you didn't, I hoped I might draw your attention to this escape route."

"We're grateful," I said. Politeness costs nothing.

"But we would like to know where you're taking us. Is it somewhere safe?" Shirin interjected.

A shrug indicated that it might be safe, or it might not, but the important part was that it was saf*er*.

"My uncle never hurt anyone who wasn't already trying to hurt him. He's respected. If he vouches for you you'll be left alone."

I hoped it was not a big 'if'.

The lift clattered to a standstill next to a ledge, many levels below where we had started. Our guide led us past astonished cargo handlers and towards the nearest outer wall. The windows only looked narrow at a distance; as we drew closer I realised that each of them could have served as a grand entrance for as imposing a palace as you could imagine. Wooden walkways had been built straight through them onto balconies clinging to the outside of the tower like bracket fungus.

Shirin caught my attention and gave me a questioning look, but I had nothing to say. I thought perhaps it would be better if we said as little as possible. Unwarranted loquaciousness could only bring problems. Our guide, at least, seemed unbothered by the lack of conversation. I resolved to emulate them.

Three sets of steps later, we arrived at a platform that turned out to be only one part of an extensive network occupying a significant breadth of the wall it was built against. It wasn't quite as full of activity as a busy port town, but it had the same sense of purpose in both the people and the space itself. Its most striking feature was a massive metal pole that poked out at least a hundred paces from the tower, held in place by thick steel stays that thrummed in the wind.

Near the top of the construction, with a commanding view of the area, was a modestly-sized hut that our escort indicated was their uncle's house.

"If this uncle is in charge of this complex, it must give him some pull," I said to Shirin, sotto voce.

"I'm more interested to know how he keeps control of it," she whispered back. "Astute political connections? His own supply of bruisers?"

I nodded. I wanted to believe this uncle had noble—or at least benign—motives, but we had to be prepared for anything.

The man who greeted us was older than I expected. He carried a smile so broad it looked like his head was about to fold in half. He shook our hands one after the other, as if he was greeting old friends.

"Yes, good! I'm glad Matija was able to find you. My name is Adetokunbo. I saw you admiring the gantry. I'm really proud of it, although it hasn't seen as much use as I had hoped."

The man was a ball of enthusiasm. Once he'd finished shaking our hands, he apparently forgot which way he'd been going and went back down the line shaking our hands again.

179

"Of course, the root problem is not the lack of demand, but the paucity of pilots. The traversal locus is hard to find in a landscape with only one visible landmark, particularly given the difficulties turbulence creates in maintaining a steady altitude. I had some idea for an apparatus I could install at the tower corners, or perhaps a more accurate tool for establishing a bearing, but then you can see the problem there, obviously. How to get the tool *back* from them?"

His whirlwind explanation left me trailing in its wake, but one detail stood out. The big pole—the 'gantry'—was a docking boom for airships. Apparently there was a second transition point out there in the sky somewhere. It must have been invaluable for those looking to trade without troubling the Cathedral authorities.

"Another possibility is a suitably accurate clock, together with the angle of the sun, but its use would be limited to daylight hours and many of our, shall we say, repeat visitors have an avowed preference for arriving and leaving at night. What approach would you recommend?"

The question came out of nowhere and hit me like a hammer. I thought I had been doing a passable job of keeping up with his patter, but I was left opening and closing my mouth like a fish.

"Signal lanterns," Garnas said, after a short pause. "Very narrow throw. They converge at the target point. The outgoing ship follows one beam out. When it crosses the second, they know they're in the proper place."

He thought for a quaver more and added:

"Pairs of lanterns in different colours, set back from each other. The relative position tells you how you need to adjust your position to get them into alignment."

Adetokunbo smacked the heel of one palm against his forehead.

"Brilliant! Brilliant and simple! I was so preoccupied with a solution that would work equally well by day and by night that I didn't consider exploiting darkness conditions."

Ah, so he was one of *those* experts. One who had sunk himself into his field purely for the love of it, and often struggled to remember that not everyone was as proficient as he was. The dedication was probably the source of his influence. He had no vulgar ambitions of his own and his expertise was simply too valuable for anyone to want to risk disrupting the status quo. He was trusted because he was fair, and he was fair because he simply didn't care about anything beyond his passion.

"I don't mean to be rude," I felt that I needed to risk a little offence if we were to point the conversation in a fruitful direction, "but we're still a little unsure what our situation is here. I can't say I'm not grateful to be taken out of reach of our... ah... welcoming committee, but it's hard to be at peace when we don't know what awaits us now."

I could almost see him shunting the technical lecture aside in his head.

"Oh, I wish I had your impeccable manners," he said, ushering us into his home.

It was as full of clutter as I had expected. The only truly clear area was in the centre, where a full size drafting table stood thick with paper. Once we were all inside he closed the door and treated us to another smile.

"Although I have manners enough not to ask how a full cantor was so much at the mercy of some cheap thugs. Unless, of course, said cantor happens to be one who has lost his voice. Quite a fascinating turn of events; I would very much like to study you but I imagine you are more concerned with doing the Cathedral council's bidding so they will fix you."

I had misjudged him. He was not oblivious to politics, but endeavouring to rise above them.

"It's not widely advertised," I said, "but it's not uncommon. Any time you attempt a Song beyond your power there's a good chance you will cause damage. Sometimes it goes away on its own, other times it requires careful treatment. If you're particularly unlucky, or were particularly foolish in your choice of Song—"

The lump in my throat brought me up short. I could feel the panic just beneath the surface, waiting for a moment when I thought about my situation just that bit too clearly.

"I see. Although it's a strange choice to send you, in particular, in pursuit of a cantor who absconded."

Garnas was about to correct him, but I shot him a look and he stayed quiet. Adetokunbo's information was not complete, then. He assumed that Cantor Cayha had run away, rather than been sent.

"This is a matter where persuasion is more likely to succeed than coercion." I decided to let him think whatever he wanted. I couldn't rule out the possibility that he would oppose us if he learned our true purpose. "Although I confess we had underestimated the other difficulties we were likely to encounter."

"Well, I can be of further help to you there. All I ask is that you allow me to accompany you as far down as you end up going."

He didn't appear to want an answer immediately. He went to one corner of the room, where a large sheet, smudged with oil and grease, hung over something. After gesturing Shirin to step slightly to one side, or at least as much as she could in the limited space, he pulled the sheet away with a flourish.

We were left staring at something that was either a small bathyscaphe or an over-sized diving suit. Or, I came to realise, something with a little of the character of both. Adetokunbo was evidently proud of it, so I assumed it was his creation.

Garnas and Shirin bore expressions of polite incomprehension. They didn't want to be rude. I had a sudden, unpleasant suspicion. I hoped I was wrong.

"I really hope you're only planning to test it. You know no-one's ever made it back. I mean no disrespect to your skills, but the others were also skilled."

His smile disappeared and was replaced by a grimace of pure determination. I wasn't wrong.

"This is a decision long in coming. I've been working towards this ever since I came to the tower. In fact, it's the *reason* I came here. I would have followed through already, but I got a little side-tracked."

I pretended not to notice how his eyes flicked sideways, to where Matija waited outside. I had begun to think of him as just another doomed soul who had heard the call of the void, but if the responsibility of a ward had held him back there was probably more to him than that. Maybe he would be the one, the first to venture into the mist's velvet embrace and return with its secrets.

I exchanged glances with the others. Garnas shrugged. Shirin tilted her head, just a little, which I recognised as her way of saying she would support whatever decision I made. In all honesty, I wasn't sure I had a choice.

"We'd be glad to have you along," I admitted. "We have a lack of local knowledge. If you can keep us from any other missteps it would be a huge help."

He winked.

"I can do better than that."

#

We laid plans to leave the following morning. Adeto-kunbo's gaff was comfortable enough a place to spend an afternoon. It might have been barely midday but I was already feeling drained. The Cathedral has a way of beating one down.

We were given the run of the gantry area, but had been warned to avoid straying too far, if only for fear of getting lost. If I sat on an outer platform, I could almost forget where I was. I wanted to forget. Before, when we were so many levels up, facing the mysterious voice and whatever had waylaid Cantor Cayha had seemed like a distant prospect. Whenever I asked myself if I was ready to face it close to, I didn't like the answer.

The gantry, at least, offered us an avenue of escape if we needed to get away from the Cathedral. I could always take my chances getting treatment elsewhere, slim as they were.

"It's alright, I'll take it to him."

I only half-heard the voices behind me. When a bowl of food was held in front of me I nodded thanks and took it automatically. We could not fault the graciousness of our host. The bowl was full of goulash, although milder than I was used to. The meat was gamy. I tried not to think too hard about how the only fauna native to the Cathedral was the common seagull.

The one who had brought me the meal had sat down next to me. We ate in silence. Once I'd finished, my companion held out a hand for the empty dish.

"Thanks," I said, but froze when I saw her face.

My would-be kidnapper smiled at me.

"Don't worry, the old man smoothed things over with my boss. Although it was funny how long it took you to notice."

I summoned up a half-hearted smile.

"Guess I must be pretty preoccupied."

184

"We've all got troubles," she said, but did not elaborate.

To our right, Matija was playing on the railing. They'd attached themselves with a safety line, but it still gave me conniptions to see someone gambolling near such a precipice.

"What'll happen to Matija? When Adetokunbo is gone?"

A shrug.

"She'll probably take over here. When she puts her mind to it, she's pretty much the same way. Less of a dreamer, maybe."

Could someone so young command the same respect? I watched the figure balanced in a crouch on a handrail. Great agility there. A silhouette of eagerness, leaning into the future.

"'She'?" I asked, doubt heavy in my voice.

A small cough. When I turned, my companion was giving me a look not of anger, but of disappointment.

"*She*. Who could possibly know better than her?"

I looked down, ashamed. Why had I stopped accepting people as they were now?

"I spoke foolishly. The Cathedral... left deeper marks on me than I knew. If I hadn't needed to come back here, well..."

"Oh, I'm sure it was a great hardship living up there, with formal dinners of imported meat and the richest cloth to wrap yourselves in."

I bit down on an angry response. There was no way she could know.

"The Cathedral authorities treat you badly because they believe you don't matter. But they believe they *own* us. There's nothing they'd do to you that they wouldn't do to us. I've seen it happen. It took everything I had—money and courage—to get away the first time."

She was quiet for a moment. Then she extended a hand.

"Apoorva."

"Eilert."

We shook. Mutual understanding had come.

"Matija was a cabin 'boy' on an airship that used to dock here. The captain had similarly rigid ideas to the Cathedral and wouldn't let her back aboard. The old man took her in without even thinking about it. He's a good person."

"Everything I've seen and heard says he is," I agreed.

"I don't feel entirely comfortable seeing him walk off with a cantor. You swear he'll be safe with you?"

"We won't hurt him. You can rely on that. I'm worried about his plan, though. If I thought I could talk him out of it, I would."

Matija had gone while we were talking, back into one of the warehouses. The afternoon was starting to cool off and it would soon be time to go indoors if I wanted to avoid the chill.

"It's been his life. Would you prefer that someone had talked you out of what you wanted for your life, persuaded you not to become a cantor?"

My answer surprised me with the speed at which it emerged.

"Yes."

#

The three of us slept on pallets in one of the working buildings. I woke up first. I've never been good at staying asleep when the sun creeps through the windows, and sleep had been elusive. Every time I had dropped off I'd been wrenched back to wakefulness by the distant voice, resonating through the stones. I could hear it, now, when everything else was quiet. It was deep into the tower; deeper than I had thought. Even then, it was clearer than the Eternal Round. When I stood up, I could see Matija looking in through the window.

I left quietly so I didn't disturb the others. I was barely through the door when Matija handed me a heavy bundle. On inspection, I saw that it was three leather overcoats wrapped around heavy masks with brass and glass goggles.

"You might as well throw away the ones you bought," she said. "Only thing they are good for is separating fools from their spending."

She froze momentarily.

"No offence meant," she added.

"And absolutely none taken," I watched her relax. "Sometimes it makes sense to let yourself be the fool. It means people are less on their guard."

She nodded, as if she was carefully filing that advice away for future consideration.

"Uncle's just about ready. Or at least, as ready as he ever gets. He's taking a few other people along as escorts. How long will your two take to get ready?"

"Shirin's military trained. Garnas is used to sleeping out in the wilderness. They're basically ready for action the moment they open their eyes. I wish I knew how they did it."

Again that thoughtful nod. She led me to where Adetokunbo was discussing the final preparations with his team. When he saw me he took my arm and led me aside.

"Our way down," he pointed.

What I had taken to be some sort of pipe grafted onto the outside of the tower turned out to be a very, very long worm gear running down as far as I could see. A platform waited invitingly for us at its top.

"I never could get it working quite properly," Adetokunbo sighed. "The torque needed to turn it was also enough to warp it. But! But I've retro-fitted a gear assembly to the platform, using the worm gear as a rack, with its own brake lever. We can ride down in style! It's just a long walk back up afterwards."

I looked at the improvised transport warily. A lot could happen between here and the bottom end. I fervently hoped that none of it involved screaming.

Our descent was jerky and uncomfortable. Several times we had to wait while the brake cooled down. Ultimately I stopped trying to follow what Adetokunbo and his crew were doing, purely for the sake of my nerves. If his aptitude for engineering failed now, there would be no saving us either way.

The platform at the bottom end was clearly in a state of disrepair; but fortunately we could step straight through one of the tower's windows from the lift itself. There were signs of construction work left abandoned; a pile of metal poles now rusted into a single lump and a toolbox long since plundered of its spanners and screwdrivers.

The bank of orange mist was closer than ever. I had always assumed that its upper boundary was mostly flat, but now I could see it had peaks and troughs. It piled up somewhat on the opposite side of the tower, following a prevailing wind that didn't exist at the top. We were on the lee side, below its uppermost billows. The air tasted sharp, unpleasant. I hurriedly put my mask on. The others had already done so.

It was profoundly unhealthy to live within the corrosive layer, and the still air inside caused it to accumulate. The only people living there were ones that had been driven out of anywhere higher. I'd seen slums before in my travels. This was worse. We were right at the very bottom of the shaft that had given me such vertigo when I'd looked down it. Looking up, there was no trace of light or colour. The platforms had been built so densely that even filth struggled to drop down to this level.

We passed groups of people huddled around lamps or cooking fires. They didn't even pretend to not be reaching for weapons, but they showed no inclination to approach us if we kept our distance. They were probably just protecting what little they had.

After some discussion amongst our expedition, Shirin took a couple of Adetokunbo's assistants and approached one of the less intimidating groups asking for information. Our rations were good barter.

"They are particularly on edge recently because someone's been attacking them, taking their food and water," Shirin explained once she had returned. "Be on the lookout for someone dressed in white."

As if we didn't have enough concerns.

"They also said that below here there are more rooms and passages. They're all empty, but it's narrow. We should mark the floor as we go to make sure we don't get lost."

She turned to me.

"Can you tell which way we should go from here?"

I shook my head. When the voice wasn't Singing, I had nothing to work with.

#

A dozen or more levels further down, Adetokunbo had us stop so he could climb inside his special suit. Air was drawn in through filters. He had prepared a supply of liquid meals he could drink through a special valve so he didn't have to open up the suit. Presumably similar measures had been taken for when he needed to evacuate himself, but I preferred not to enquire.

Not long after, however, it seemed as though the mist was getting *less* dense, rather than more. The strangeness of the entire situation preyed on our minds so much that we were caught flat-footed when we turned a corner and came face to face with a figure in white.

I saw the truth of it quickly. The cut of a cantor's attire is distinctive, even when foul vapours have leached all the colour out of it.

"Cantor Cayha?" I spoke quickly, before anyone could panic. "We were asked to look for you."

I hoped beginning with that would make us appear concerned rather than a threat. I opened the heavy coat just enough to show my own clothes to her.

"I don't want any trouble," I added.

I put myself in front of the others. I guessed she'd be more reluctant to attack a fellow cantor.

"And I don't want anyone to get hurt." I licked my dry lips. "We're just here to find out what's going on."

"If the council sent you—" I could hear dangerous harmonics gathering in her voice as she spoke.

"I can't Sing any more," I took the risk of interrupting her. "That's why they sent me. I'm expendable."

She came closer, and stared through the glass of my mask.

"I know you. A baritone. You left. Why are you back?"

"To see if they can cure me. The council left it unsaid that they wouldn't let me see the cantors medica unless I came down here. They're worried. You know the calamity a wild talent might cause—"

"You don't know what you're talking about," she said hotly. "You've not heard him. He's more than an untrained cantor.

Much more. Sometimes I think instead of him Singing to the universe, it Sings *through* him."

She appeared to reach a decision.

"He'll start his next piece soon. I'll allow you to listen. Then you'll understand. If any of you try anything—*anything*—I'll Sing you apart where you stand."

I had no doubt she could.

She ducked through an archway, waved us to follow. I gestured for Adetokunbo, his ward and team to stay put. No sense bringing them into danger.

She took us into a chamber, one almost identical to the many others we'd passed through. Water dribbled into fœtid puddles and through cracks in the masonry. There was the functional minimum of an encampment set up near the centre. Two bedrolls, some blankets, the ashes of a cooking fire and some crates to sit on. It was all centred on a man, one who was kneeling directly on the floor despite the crates.

He looked to be in his thirties, but he was so emaciated and world-worn he could have been much younger. Rags hung off his sparse frame. He was staring upwards at the featureless ceiling. Was he really the one we were looking for?

Songs were magic. They could do just about anything. We cantors had been taught Songs that, in extremis, could halt starvation. It was a horrible way to live day to day, and you could never Sing away the *feeling* of hunger, but you could survive. I guessed that was how the stranger had lived until Cayha had found him. It wasn't possible to Sing away thirst, however. Your mouth dried out quicker than you could replenish fluids. The blisters on his lips, just starting to heal, told me he'd been licking the tainted water dripping down the walls.

Cayha misinterpreted my examination and started to take a deep breath.

"Easy now," I said, resisting the urge to back away. "I can see you've been taking care of him."

"There's not much proper food around here. The sub-cisterns don't want to part with it."

Taken without thinking, with the arrogance of power. Some habits of the Cathedral ran deep.

"It's time," she added. "We'll talk afterwards."

I looked down at the wretched man, sitting in his filthy rags and staring into nothing.

He began to Sing.

I had been taught that folk singing was a lesser art, but I wasn't so blinkered as to have deafened myself to the reality outside the Cathedral's authority. Music was a source of joy, a way of bringing people together and a way for one person to let their raw emotion rasp against the feelings of others. It had purpose and it had value, even when reality didn't Sing along.

What I listened to now was a perfect fusion of both. Harmonics tickled my cantor's senses. I could feel the delicate strings of the universe being plucked with utmost precision by a craftsman beyond any I had heard before, but I could also hear the bravura performance of a virtuoso hedge singer, summoning up memories I'd thought lost. The distinction between the two faded until I could barely even think of them as separate ideas. All the universe was gathered at a point of perfect sound and I was powerless in its grip.

Tendrils of mist in the corners of the room were pushed back, returning through the very cracks they'd seeped in through. The mist also swirled out around and behind us, through the passage. He was Singing it away. I had to fight my urge to Sing with him.

Eventually, the man fell silent. Whatever power was in him lay dormant again.

I wept. I don't know for how long.

Shirin gently shook me back to myself. She didn't need to ask if I was okay; her expression did that for her.

"I'm fine," I lied.

I took a few more moments to gather myself.

"I can't let the Cathedral destroy this," I said, as much to confirm my own feelings as to tell anyone else.

Cantor Cayha looked at me. She'd tried to tell me. I hadn't understood.

"The council won't let this go," I told her. "They will send more people down here."

"I will fight them."

"That won't help."

She started to reply but I held up a hand. Was there a way to finesse this? I pressed my hand to the cold floor, then lay down so I could do the same with my ear. The Eternal Round was just at the limit of my hearing.

Cayha reached out her hand as well. I could see her mouthing along with it. Her senses were clearly keener than mine.

"Teach him," I said, after inspiration came. "Let him Sing along with the Round from time to time. If he's working to strengthen it, that might mollify the council. I'll do what I can to dissuade them from sending anyone else here."

She nodded slowly. Anything that preserved the man's Song would be fine by her, I could see.

"Learn how he suppresses the mist. You'll live longer."

She was one of the Maestra Soprano's finest. If anyone could...

"The people around here are just scared of you," Shirin said. "You don't have to hurt them."

Garnas gestured to the anonymous singer.

"Maybe he can sing away the mist over a wider area? If you can open up the rooms around here people will have better shelter. Ask them to give you a little food as thanks. Then you're working together. They'll probably even warn you if more cantors turn up."

Cayha was thinking about the idea, at least. I didn't want to push her too far. Her exposure to this man's Song had made her unpredictable.

Shirin whispered to me: "Is there anything else we should do?"

I knew her well enough to know that her hand would be subtly moving towards her axe. What she was really asking was if we needed to take the other cantor down. I'd seen Shirin's skill first hand, but an axe was a poor weapon to take up against Song.

"I think it's going to be okay," I said.

It was largely out of our hands, anyway. We'd done what the council had asked us to do. I had the rest of the journey to concoct a story that would keep them from probing further.

Cantor Cayha gestured impatiently for us to leave. I gave her a nod and a smile, then we returned to the others.

#

It was late in the day, by Adetokunbo's timepiece, when the mist grew thick again. We'd descended so many more levels, empty staircase after empty staircase, that we simply didn't care to count how many there had been. The guards who had come with us were getting restless. It would be a terrible thing to have to spend the night down there. I think their discomfort was ultimately what led to Adetokunbo bringing us to a halt.

"I think the rest of you have come far enough. It's time to say goodbye. I've never been very good at speeches."

He considered what he'd just said.

"At least, I've never been very good at speeches other people listened to. So I'll just offer my thanks. It might feel like you didn't do all that much, but I know better."

He shook everyone's hand, even Matija's, with careful solemnity. Then, awkwardly, he raised a hand in goodbye and set off on his own. I followed for a few paces, one hand on the wall. The mist was thick enough for me to be sure I didn't want to lose my bearings. I put the other on the shoulder of Adetokunbo's bulky suit.

"Are you sure you want to go through with this?" I asked.

"Positively."

"Even if it means never coming back? Matija will miss you," I felt like a villain bringing her into it, but I knew I'd never quite forgive myself if I didn't at least remind him of what he was leaving behind.

"I know," he sighed. "It would be nice to stay. But if I wait any longer I'll be too old to go. It's now or never. Matija understands, I think."

I pulled my hand back. I'd already known it wasn't an impulsive decision, but now I knew he'd made it clear-eyed.

"How far down will you go?"

He took another step, the mist enveloping him in an almost liquid way.

"I'll go on until I can be absolutely sure that no-one has ever been so deep before. Then I'll come back."

He wouldn't, I realised. What could possibly satisfy his condition? Unless there really was ground down there somewhere and his suit survived long enough for him to reach it. I was witnessing a legend in the making.

"Goodbye, then."

He waved a hand in response. Only a few steps later he slipped out of sight.

I couldn't see if Matija was crying under her mask. If she was, then let her. There was no shame in it.

Then there was only the long ascent.

#

I don't remember all that much from the following few days. So many steps and so much time taken to climb them. Whenever there was no immediate focus for my attention, my mind would drift back to the Song. Maybe a part of me is still in that room.

Matija grew with the journey. She started to hold her head higher, keep her back straighter. By the time we reached her uncle's workshops she was issuing instructions and watching them be followed. Acceptance and respect is how you allow people to reach their full potential. Discipline is how you manufacture obedient servants.

#

"It was serendipitous to send me, in particular. Not to mention my assistants."

It was better to call them such in front of the council. They were unused to thinking of people who could not Sing as equals. I was glad the Maestro Bass was absent. It meant there were only three people to pick my story apart.

"They needed to drag me away. If I had been in full voice, I would have Sung their ruin so I could keep listening."

"Is it really so bewitching?" Maestra Katka leaned forwards.

196

"Cantor Cayha never left. If she couldn't overcome it..."

I wanted to engender just the right amount of fear. Let them think that the more powerful the cantor, the greater the hazard. They had to be dissuaded from sending any more cantors but not induced to see the man as an existential threat. In truth, I doubted anyone else would be as captivated as Cayha was. I suspect she was a special case, a product of Katka's abuses.

"The good news is that I believe the Eternal Round is safe. Before I left I was able to teach some of it to the man. He is so much a prisoner to his own music that I don't believe he's even able to think of disrupting it."

The last part was true, at least. I thought about adding more, but opted not to. The less I said, the less there was to have holes poked in it.

"Would you say that interfering with him would be more dangerous than leaving him be?" Maestro Athol asked.

I sensed the question might be a trap.

"That's up to the council's judgement," I shrugged. "I wouldn't want to make the decision."

"I suppose that if there must be a rogue voice down the tower then it's better to be one kept benign," Dieuwke said. "We have enough other matters to attend to."

Katka looked unconvinced, but when she looked to Athol for support he shook his head. I think he only cared about establishing that the strange Song wasn't part of one of his rival's plans.

"The council thanks you for your assistance," he said, making his decision clear, "and it hopes you make a full recovery."

I bowed, as deeply as I felt I could without looking sarcastic, and backed out of the chamber. As the doors began to close, Dieuwke caught my eye, and in the final quavers before they were fully shut she gave me a small nod of approval. I wish I knew why.

#

The senior cantor medica took his time assessing me. After listening to my throat with his stethoscope, he brought a lens in front of a candle and bid me open wide. He Sang softly to himself to assess the damage. I was impatient for him to finish his inspection. Not knowing was torture.

"How did you injure your voice?" he asked.

"I was reaching for a *Fulgur Percutiens* in panic. I Sang up *something*, but it wasn't a clean single bolt. Quite a tangle of them."

He straightened up sharply. After checking that we were still alone, he said:

"My advice to you is to never repeat that. What you're describing is not a botched *Fulgur Percutiens* but an actualised *Fulgur Tempestatis*. There's only one other person alive who's successfully Sung it."

He gestured for me to open my mouth again and I obeyed.

"The council doesn't like anyone wielding that kind of power. They manipulated her into filling the empty council seat, the better to keep her under observation."

He looked me dead in the eyes.

"Yes, to reach blindly all the way past the *Percutiens* and accidentally Sing a *Tempestatis*, well, it's a wonder you didn't explode. I'd expect only the most powerfully gifted to pull it off."

The rest of the examination was conducted in silence. I had questions I wanted to ask; but as the breves ticked by

I realised that he would not answer them. He'd given me a warning and I would be a fool to ignore it.

"Good news," he said. "There is no permanent damage done. A few medicinal verses a day and you should be well on the path to recovery. Even so, it would be best to avoid Singing outside your register for a couple of months."

He wiped his hands on his apron. I was so relieved I felt my eyes start to water.

"But above all, avoid the Song that caused the injury."

The Arenose Eternity

The airship died in splinters, dashing itself against the dunes in fury at its fate. The gasbag, tatters now, snapped its last line and was dragged back into the pitiless sky. People, scattered like leaves, picked themselves up and fought disbelief that they had survived. The ones who had not been so lucky stayed where they had been thrown.

Garnas had little more than bruises. Like the other passengers, he had been in the aft of the gondola, the better to survive the impact. Fortune had favoured him with respect to injury and it was time to take stock of their situation. Help those that could be helped. Of his immediate companions, Eilert was as groggy as he was but Shirin was already on her feet and searching the wreckage. Of the other three passengers, only one had survived. The elderly couple had been too fragile to weather the impact.

It struck him as a cruel fate. The couple had only gone to Caelum Cathedrale in hope that the cantors medica would deign to help with the wasting disease they had contracted. The Cathedral had rebuffed them without compassion, a blow so crushing they had taken passage on the first vessel scheduled to leave, heedless of destination. To have perished in this accident was an indignity unworthy of the love they had shared.

The crew had fought with the dying ship to the last, slowing its descent and flattening its trajectory. Putting themselves at greater risk to preserve the passengers, even though the crew out-numbered them. It was the least those passengers could do to return the favour.

Eilert found the captain.

"Parsan! Are you still with us?"

"Death couldn't possibly hurt this much," the captain replied. "It's me arm."

The ship's wheel had been thrown together with the captain, whose arm was between the spokes and clearly broken. Eilert went to search the debris for something to splint the arm before trying to free it.

Garnas saw the captain needed no extra help, so he headed straight for the largest fragment of the airship. A forest of sharp metal edges tore at his clothes as he climbed into it, calling.

"Yazhu!"

A groan guided him to the remains of an interior cabin. The airship had been lightweight, so it didn't take much effort to heave aside one of the large wall panels from where it had collapsed inwards. The stricken figure Garnas exposed had been gravely hurt by the wall, despite its flimsiness.

"I came here for the ship's compass," the victim explained. "It's the only one aboard that'll work in this messed up magnetic field. I reckoned we'd need it."

They stretched out an arm, half-heartedly. Just beyond their fingers, a shattered metal case spilled viscous fluid and gears out onto the sand.

"I'm more worried about you," Garnas said. "Where does it hurt?"

"Where *doesn't* it hurt?" The chuckle turned into a damp moan.

Garnas got no response when he tested Yazhu's arms and legs, but the hiss of pain when he pressed gently on the ribs suggested a break. It was not an encouraging sign. Moving the injured would ordinarily be considered an error, but there was no alternative here. Garnas used the wall panel as a makeshift sled and pulled Yazhu onto it, as gently as he could. Every gasp of pain he heard cut through him like a knife. Once they were on the sled, he used some spare rope to fashion a rough harness he could use to pull it.

Eilert finished splinting the captain's arm and watched Garnas laboriously drag Yazhu over to where the survivors had assembled.

Four passengers, five crew. Apart from the officers—Captain Parsan and navigator Ruan Yazhu—three ratings had lived. Able seaman Cadoc was a giant of a man who looked like he could pull himself out of the wreckage of anything. The other two, Vsevolod and Massey, stood in his shadow, literally and figuratively. Massey had a bloody nose. The other surviving passenger was Kurchivie, a salamander-like humanoid on what he had called a pilgrimage. When Shirin pointed out that one of his fingers was badly mangled, he tutted, snapped it off his hand and threw it away.

"It'll grow back," he explained, "if enough time is given to it."

Agitation grew. In the immediate aftermath of the crash there had been no space for it. Now, however, there was time for the leaden realisation of their predicament to settle. Something had gone awry with the transition out of the interstice, leaving the airship foundering from the moment it had arrived in the world. Its intended destination had been a town called The Pinch, the only settlement for hundreds of miles in any direction, and days distant over trackless desert. There was scant hope that another vessel would overfly them soon enough to matter.

Captain Parsan climbed onto a piece of debris, the better to project calm authority.

"I've flown over this desert dozens of times. There's absolutely nothing here. No oases, no paths, no scrubland. The nearest source of food and water is The Pinch." The captain could not quite keep his fatalism out of his voice. "We make it there safely, or we die." He licked his lips while he waited for his words to sink in. "I know a lot about flying, but nothing about trekking over land."

All eyes turned to Garnas. He was the closest they had to an expert. A desert was very different to a jungle, but some basics were unchanged.

"Drinking water is going to be our biggest problem," Garnas said. "We must conserve as much of it as we can, and that starts *now*."

He tied a cloth over his nose and mouth, demonstrating how to minimise water loss through breath.

"Take sips, and only when you absolutely have to. It's better to reach safety joking about how much water we still had left than die with safety in sight because we wasted it. The sooner you restrict your intake, the sooner your body will adjust. Don't worry too much about food. We'll die of thirst before hunger becomes a real problem."

He looked around, noting who nodded immediately and who appeared reluctant. He could feel his skin tingling where the sun beat down on it.

"We should rest during the day. The nights are going to be colder than you think, but if we keep moving we should stay warm enough. Do not wander off alone, not for anything. If you lose sight of the group you may never find it again. You can't trust your sense of direction."

He turned to the captain.

"How do we find The Pinch?"

Parsan scratched his chin.

"We usually just put on altitude until we can see it."

Yazhu coughed. They levered themselves up onto their elbows.

"The bearing is north-north-east," they croaked. "You can take it from the sun, but the stars are useless here. Magnetic compasses, too; something about the desert. We only need to get close enough for someone to see us and they'll send help."

They looked like they wanted to say more, but didn't have the strength.

Eilert spoke up.

"There's a Song that shows where the sun will rise next. Keep us on track at night."

#

There was still some time before sunset, time enough to gather what they could from the wreckage. The water barrels, those still intact, were too heavy to carry, but bottles and canteens could be filled from them. Every available receptacle was pressed into service. The fortunate find of part of the gasbag would, in combination with some struts, become a bivouac to shield them from the sun.

The captain argued with Cadoc over a crate of ship's biscuits. Food, but barely edible without water to soften them. Captain Parsan insisted they would only make them thirstier. Heated words were exchanged until Cadoc was told that if he wanted to take them, no-one would help him carry them. It was too hot for the argument to last. Much of the crate's contents ended up shoved into pockets and bags by Cadoc and his hangers-on.

The heat stayed in the air well after night had fallen. They trudged in single file in the stale air of twilight. Garnas was at the rear, doing his best to match pace with the others as he dragged Yazhu's sled behind him. The sky was scattered with stars, far more than he was used to. Even the interstice couldn't match it for density and colour. There was nothing one could hang a frame of reference on, so rich and deep was the star field. No denser band of light, no moon hanging low and red. More startling still was the speed with which the stars moved. It owed nothing to the passage of day and night, or to the slow precession of seasons. They raced the night itself, dashing over every degree of arc they could before dawn washed them away. Navigating with them would have been folly.

They made good time to start with, but fine sand is a hellish surface to walk on for any length of time and as the night wore on the pace slackened. Short breaks for rest and sips of water did little to rejuvenate any of them. Captain Parsan had planned on continuing through dawn until the heat became too much, but he had to admit defeat as the eastern sky began to glow. Thanks to the difference in clock times between worlds they had all been awake well over thirty-six hours. To try and keep spirits up, he passed the early stop off as a precaution in case setting up the canvas awning proved troublesome.

Without a word, Garnas unslung the sled's ropes from around himself and stretched. He'd given most of his nominal water ration to Yazhu, whose condition had not improved. He told himself that he was more used to living lean in the wilderness, but he couldn't deny, even to himself, that taking so little water was unsustainable.

Cadoc and his cronies weren't making any attempt to help make camp. Garnas sighed, took one of the poles and pushed it into the sand. It stuck on something, and no amount of wiggling would sink it any further. He used his hands to dig a shallow hole, and was shocked when he brought up bones. Whole, for the most part, and long scoured clean of any flesh. He dug around further and found that the bones seemed to lie in a thick layer not far beneath the surface, everywhere he searched.

Alarmed shouts from around the camp told him that others were making the same unwelcome discovery. The sand was pale, almost ivory. Garnas held his fingers up to his eyes, studying the grains stuck to their tips. They *could* be powdered bone. He went to taste them but stopped short, preferring not to know.

The awning afforded too little space to offer any real privacy. Habit dissuaded them from huddling together and there was considerable passive-aggressive jockeying for position before they settled. Despite their weariness, it was hard to rest under the bright light of the sun. The air was oven-hot and pitiless. Around noon, Parsan and Shirin had to move to the other side of the shelter, as the shadow had moved and exposed them to the day's full heat.

Shirin stayed awake for a while. Deserts might exemplify a place with no people, but it was hard to rest when she knew no watch was posted. Eilert was face down on his folded up coat, drooling into his mask. Garnas had curled up at the foot of Ruan Yazhu's improvised litter.

Shirin was worried for the both of them. They had been inseparable from the moment Garnas boarded the airship, intoxicated by each others' company. Even if romance didn't bloom, they were likely to become fast friends for life. There was an ease of trust, a depth of understanding that belied the short time they'd known each other. And now, one of them was gravely ill and the other in a state of premature mourning. Shirin had seen some people handle anticipation of loss worse, seen many more handle it better. There was not much she could do for either of them until the immediate danger had passed. She had never developed much skill with words, and words were what was needed.

\#

It was only the second night and already it felt like they had fallen into a pattern. Conservation of water demanded that they spoke as little as possible, and exertion made it mandatory. The desert was not entirely quiet; the occasional mysterious hooting noise carried from somewhere far in the distance, and every now and again a great crack, as if two heavy rocks had been struck together, followed it. The wind rasping against the edges of the dunes had its own timbre, background noise that swallowed the sounds of their feet as they kicked up sand.

The shifting starscape lent an air of unreality to their labour. It was hard to dislodge the idea that it was a dream, one on the brink of tipping into a nightmare, that could vanish in a moment when they were jolted out of slumber.

When, now and again, Eilert used his cantor's magic to check they were heading in the right direction, it provided a welcome moment of relative normalcy.

#

Captain Parsan acknowledged defeat long before noon. As cold as the night remained just before the sun reappeared over the horizon, the temperature climbed sharply afterwards. Five attempts to get the gasbag remnant correctly hoisted and they were prepared to live with one corner drooping badly. Sleep found them quickly this time, aided by their exhaustion, and experience had taught them where to lie so they would stay in the shade all through the day.

The sun wasn't even fully below the horizon that evening when shouting echoed over the desert.

"I warned you about the biscuits." Parsan stood over Cadoc. "If you're thirsty, that's your own fault. It's not fair to strong-arm other people out of their water."

"I really don't mind—" Kurchivie stammered, clutching a glass bottle to his chest and leaning away from them both.

"I won't allow it," Parsan insisted.

"You're not the captain any more." Snarling, Cadoc was on his feet in a flash. "There's no ship. You got us into this mess and I won't let you order me around!"

"I don't want to order anyone around." Parsan couldn't keep the anger out of his tone as he squared up to the larger man. "We're in this together and we have to be fair. What would you have done differently?"

"Dead weight should have been left behind," Cadoc said.

He didn't look at Ruan Yazhu's stretcher. He didn't need to. Garnas was halfway to his feet, spoiling for a fight despite Eilert's warning hand on his arm. Vsevolod kept a contemptuous eye on him while Massey stood shoulder-to-shoulder with Cadoc.

Parsan took a step towards Cadoc, keeping himself between him and the others. Shirin hovered just behind his shoulder, her face impassive.

"Please, Cadoc," the captain pleaded. "You're not thinking clearly. We're all at our limit right now. Take a moment to—"

"You're telling me what to do again!" A knife appeared in Cadoc's hand and he took a threatening step—

He folded up around Shirin's axe, grunting quietly as if in surprise. She'd moved so quickly, and struck with such precision, he'd been able to offer no counter. His gasp turned into a gurgle. It had been a killing blow. Only now did Shirin's face show emotion: her features twisted with distaste at what she'd had to do.

Cadoc fell to the ground when she pulled her weapon away. Everyone but Shirin found it hard to look away from where the blood flowed into the sand. Not with disgust, not even with horror, but with sadness at all the moisture going to waste.

The dead man's lackeys were quiet. They were prepared to ride the coattails of a trouble-maker but not to make trouble on their own account. The passivity in their eyes made it plain they wouldn't fight any more. At least, not while Shirin and her axe factored into matters.

The silence was heavy that night. No-one felt like breaking it, even when they set up camp. They lay down practically in one pile, all habits of personal space forgotten. Fitful rest was the best they could expect; they welcomed it. Even Shirin overcame her reluctance to sleep unguarded.

#

Ruan Yazhu died while the others slept.

#

Captain Parsan, who had known the navigator the longest, gave a short eulogy. There was not much to be said that would not ring hollow. The desert wind scoured away the delusions of civilisation, leaving only the bare truth. Words bunched in Garnas's throat. Words he was desperate to say but couldn't, and words he knew he shouldn't say, threatening to burst out of his mouth anyway. No attempt was made to bury Yazhu's remains. The old bones lay too shallowly under the surface. The only reverence that could be enacted was to cover the body. The desert would consume Ruan Yazhu as completely as worms would.

As the heat haze on the horizon dissipated, a dark line was visible across the sand to the east. It was, to the best of everyone's knowledge, not there when they had made camp. Whatever it proved to be, they could not afford a detour.

Two hours into the night, under the gaze of the wheeling stars, a gentle susurration rolled across the dunes. It grew louder as the dark band drew closer. It was only when they were almost on top of it that the truth was evident.

It was a marching column of beetles. The largest among them was as big as a hand, the shine on their carapaces hidden under a patina of desert dust. The front of the column was out of sight, over the horizon. The rearguard was closer, close enough that Parnas made the decision to take a short rest and wait for the insects to pass.

Garnas sat alone, unsure exactly what he was feeling. Losing someone he cared about, someone he might even have come to love, was almost too hard to bear; but had he really earned such a keen sense of loss for someone he had barely met? Was it because of what they had meant to him, or because it had injured his pride to have been unable to save them? Guilt that he had been asleep, rather than at Yazhu's side, burned hotly inside him, and no amount of rationalisation about exhaustion drove it out of his head. Worst of all were bitter thoughts that it would have been better to have left Yazhu at the crash site, and not tire himself out dragging them. He wanted to rage, to fight something or to scream his feelings at the uncaring sky, but he didn't have the strength for either.

He heard the shouting before he noticed the sand boiling underneath him. He was barely to his feet when a scorpion as long as his arm shook the last of the sand away and scurried towards the beetle caravan.

The same was happening all over. Ambush predators, lying in wait beneath the surface, woken by the arrival of prey. Why they had emerged now, and not earlier, could only be guessed at.

Nowhere was safe. Any patch of sand could erupt into scorpions without warning. Bones, disturbed by the digging of the arachnids, poked out of the sand at odd angles. Vsevolod tried to limp away, blood streaming down one calf. Eilert sang a song of protection while Shirin called out for everyone to gather around the cantor. Garnas put his shoulder under Vsevolod's arm and helped him towards safety.

The beetles, panicked, ran in all directions. The footing became treacherous, and a fall risked putting one's face on the level of the scorpions' stingers.

The ridge of the dune collapsed under Garnas's feet. With his last effort he pushed Vsevolod within reach of the others, who hauled him to safety as Garnas fell back. He landed further than he expected, and harder, just in time to see the blurred jumble of bones, sand and scorpions as it buried him.

#

He awoke somewhere unexpectedly cool.

The darkness he took to be night, before remembering that no night here would be so dark. It was black as pitch, with no glimmer of even reflected light. Long habit led his hand to the waxed box of matches in a belt pouch, and the flare of one left after-images dancing across his eyes. His head hurt, but a quick personal inventory told him he had no obvious impairments. He was lying on solid rock, either worn or polished smooth. He'd seen no solid ground since the airship crash; so he presumed he had been carried some distance while he had been insensible. A cave, perhaps, or an underground passageway. Nothing told him which way might lead him back out into the open air, or back to the others.

A sense of unease drove him into a crouch. The air was stuffy, almost stale. This did not feel like a place of safety. Anything could have happened to their desperate band in the interim. A distant tapping, like a cane on stone, became discernible. As the sound drew louder and closer he pulled a knife from his belt. His long gun was nowhere to be seen by meagre match-light. A pool of light presaged the newcomer and Garnas extinguished his match with a quick shake. He might need the advantage of ambush.

The lantern, held high, threw light into every corner of the cave.

Garnas pressed himself against the cave wall, knuckles white around the handle of his knife. The bearer of the lantern was nothing but a skeleton, a fleshless simulacrum whose empty eye sockets carried a piercing gaze. Garnas waited for an attack from it, or for the jolt of an awakening from a nightmare, but neither came.

The skeleton had noticed him, but it was doing nothing. Or, Garnas came to think, it was waiting for his terror to subside. A knife was of little use against an enemy with no flesh for it to bite into. He forced himself to breathe more slowly. The fear could not be entirely dispelled, but there seemed to be no immediate danger. He tucked the knife back into his sheath.

The skeleton moved then, but slowly. It took a couple of steps over to him, then crouched down to offer him a hand up.

He swallowed hard. His own hand shook despite his best efforts but the skeleton's grip was gentle, if firm. Once he had been helped to his feet, the skeleton inclined its head, perhaps in greeting. The lantern cast flickering shadows even though it had no flame burning in it. Where one would expect to see wick and oil, there was only a shimmering

green glow in which there were, intermittently, vague silhou-
ettes.

Garnas considered the possibility that his wits had been
scrambled by the blow to his head. Recent events made no
sense, but apart from the overt bizarreness there was no
dreamlike quality to what he saw. Even if he was in the grip
of a delusion, he could scarcely do anything other than play
along with it.

The skeleton beckoned him back down the tunnel. The
rock walls were more than smooth, Garnas realised, they
were polished. The floor, too, although there were signs that
the passage of untold numbers of feet had worn dimples in
the otherwise finished surface. Or, if not many feet, then the
same feet many, many times. The tunnel led into a wider
cave, one where torches burned in high sconces with the
same unnatural light as the lantern.

An empty dais lay along one wall. It gave no clue as to
what it had once borne. The wall behind it was filled with a
triptych frieze. The skeleton invited Garnas to examine it.

The carvings were highly stylised, presenting a jumbled
perspective that tried to show all sides of its subjects in a
single panel. The first showed a figure recumbent on a bed.
No, a bier. The figure was dying, alone. The second showed
a road, winding through darkness. The figure was no longer
alone, but with a companion. The companion was holding
a lantern, one whose rays cut through every other detail in
the image. With a little imagination, its shape was reminiscent of the one carried by the skeleton. The final panel was
a jumble of contradicting pictures, like a mirror had been
smashed and the pieces put back in place in such a way
that each reflected a different world; an arboreal paradise, a
storm-tossed sea, rolling plains and others Garnas could not
identify.

His upbringing had not included any religious component. It was something important to other people, not his own. He doubted that even the inhabitants of The Pinch would be familiar with this; this faith had the feel of something old and forgotten by everything except itself. The shape of it was not unknown to him; he'd learned that the idea of a persona to guide the dead was not uncommon.

The skeleton might have been holding its lamp a little higher when he turned away from the triptych, or it could have been his imagination.

They were both guides, he realised. He for a jungle few had cause to visit, and the skeleton for the final path everyone would walk, in time. With the revelation came a sense of peace, an unwinding of the anxiety that had been twisted into him since the crash. Death often came with pain and misery, but it didn't have to be so. The frieze's story was not a warning, nor was it melancholy. The end of life could be seen as just another facet of it, without judgement.

It would not be so bad to enter an afterlife where he could speak with Ruan Yazhu again. They had parted too soon. Maybe even, if the hope was not forlorn, he would find his parents there. He had no confirmation that they had died—and probably never would—but he had spent half his life in acceptance of never seeing them again. If death had been forced on him, Garnas could face whatever came afterwards with courage, even if what came next was nothing.

He followed the skeleton into another room, his steps quieter than he expected. This place felt less grand, less sacred, with another tunnel leading onwards. A crack in the wall permitted a trickle of water to flow into a small basin carved out the rock itself. The water flowed clear. The skeleton gestured for Garnas to approach it. After spending so long surviving on cracked lips and willpower it looked ambrosial. He drank from his canteens first, water he knew to be good, then brought cupped hands from the basin to his mouth. It was the coldest thing he had ever tasted.

His own thirst slaked, he carefully filled his water bottles. His personal canteen was somewhat oversized, as much a veteran of the jungle as he was. He waited patiently for it to fill and watched the bubbles spin across the water.

The skeleton would not have brought him here, he was sure, if it had ill intent. He'd assumed his arrival in its domain was the result of his injury, directly or indirectly. Limbo between the living and the dead. Although the feeling was not completely dispelled, the presence of something as mundane as fresh water brought him comfort. Or maybe the passageways between life and death were always coincident with a place you could find on a map.

He became aware of a feeling of gravity, as if something truly significant had occurred that he had only noticed once it was passed. A choice made.

The tunnel ahead, which he had taken as the natural next destination, now looked... wrong. Not sinister, as such, but unsuitable for him in a way that defied explanation. Something he had done, maybe, had closed it off to him. Or some solemn intelligence had judged him unworthy.

A choice made? The sound of the water seemed to grow louder.

When the skeleton held its lantern close to it, it turned into a flow of sand. When it was drawn away, it became water again. Even the sound changed. When it was water, it was a thing of life. When it was sand, it was a thing of death.

A choice? There had not truly been any choice at all. Without even thinking, Garnas had taken water not for himself but for the others. He was a guide through and through.

The skeleton tilted its head at him. An acknowledgement perhaps, from one specialist to another. When it lifted its lamp, a new tunnel was revealed in the cave wall. Perhaps it had been there all along.

His steps along that tunnel felt *right*, in a way he could not understand. Each stride he took felt like there were miles passing under him. Distance without speed. When it opened into dry night air, the painted sky drifting overhead, the change was sudden.

The skeleton went no further than the mouth of the tunnel. It gestured for him to go, not with urgency but with the patience of aeons. He nodded to it, a gesture of thanks that he was sure would be understood, and crossed the threshold.

It did not surprise him in the least that the tunnel was not there when he turned around. Nor was there any bare rock that could now mask the tunnel entrance. He was back on the seemingly endless sands. And there, only a hundred yards away, were Shirin, Eilert, Parsan and the rest.

They were just stirring from sleep. Kurchivie did a double take when he saw Garnas, shouting so the others could confirm what he didn't quite believe.

Eilert ran to him and gave him a hug so fierce it lifted him off his feet.

"I knew that if anyone could find us again, it would be you," the cantor said, tears in his eyes.

"We couldn't get down to where you'd fallen, thanks to those damnable scorpions," Captain Parsan explained. "All we could do was get some distance from them. We tarried as long as we dared but when you didn't make your own way to us, we assumed the worst."

"*Some* of us assumed the worst," Eilert corrected.

"You'll be needing this." Shirin handed Garnas his long gun, recovered from the mayhem.

Even Vsevolod was there. The scorpions' venom, he explained, was evidently harmless to humans.

After the excitement of the reunion, Garnas had a chance to look at them properly. He was shocked at how they had deteriorated—every cheek was sunken, all skin like paper. They were equally amazed with how healthy he looked in comparison.

"You've been missing for four days," Parsan said, shortly. "How did you even find us?"

"If I told you, you would probably think I'd lost my mind."

Garnas unslung his water bottles and offered them around.

"You need this more than I do."

They were too thirsty to ask where he'd found water. He made sure they didn't drink it all at once.

"You want me to take point?" he asked Parsan.

"Please."

Before the night ended, they saw another dark band on the horizon. This one was unmistakably a rocky ridge, running north to south with a single cleft directly ahead. The town of The Pinch lay in that cleft. Safety was in sight.

Eilert sang up a column of red light, an arcane firework, and it exploded over their heads with a crack. Unless every eye in The Pinch was turned away, someone would know people were stranded in the desert. It would not be hard to connect it to the airship's failure to arrive on schedule.

#

They were woken by the sound of a gyrocopter just after noon. It was the spotter for the rescue party, who arrived not long afterwards. They had come with extra camels, two doctors and, of course, plenty of food and water. It didn't even matter that the last few miles to safety were travelled under the full glare of the sun.

#

Their survival was heralded as a miracle in The Pinch. The upper desert, on the opposite side, had regular trade caravans criss-crossing it. The lower desert was held to be an ill-omened place, untravelled except in emergencies. Even then, only with reluctance. Recovering even one lost soul from it was a once-a-decade tale.

The Pinch itself was a sight to behold. The two deserts were at dramatically different elevations, and the notch in the ridge of mountains was the only place where one could spill into the other. A cascade of sand fell two hundred feet, draining so much like an hourglass that The Pinch had been named for one. Central to the town was its bridge, an essential link in the road running north to south along the mountains.

Before embarking on the fateful voyage, the passengers had been warned that accommodation and food was unusually expensive in The Pinch, a consequence of its limited resources. It transpired that rescuees were treated very differently. Seven different local families each took in one survivor, fed them for free, and nursed them back to health. It would be several weeks before the next airship was due to arrive, time enough to make a full recovery.

"The desert is the enemy," the head of one of the families said, explaining the distinction to Garnas and Parsan.

"Like the law of the sea," the captain said. "You help a vessel in distress, no matter what."

The three of them stood on the bridge over the flowing sand. It was almost narrow enough to jump across, but it ran so swiftly that to fall into it was to never resurface.

"What will you do now?" Garnas asked.

Parsan shrugged.

"Yazhu gave me their rutter. I can probably use it to get a navigator's position on another ship. Maybe save up enough for a part share of a new ship." He paused. "I think they knew they weren't going to make it."

Garnas nodded slowly.

"Did I do the right thing? Not trying to save them, I mean, so much as putting myself so much at risk trying to do so. It can't have been easy for them to watch."

"I think..." the captain trailed off.

"I think," he tried again, "that spending just a few more days with you, even in those circumstances, was what they wanted. They trusted you to know your limits."

"More than they should have," Garnas muttered, but he smiled.

The family head nodded.

"The holy books tell us that everyone who dies in the desert becomes a star in the sky. Your friend will be in good company here. I'll say a prayer to their memory whenever I can."

Garnas thought of cold bones under the sand, and silent caves.

"We all came close to joining them, that's a fact." Parsan shuddered. "No disrespect meant, but I'm happier to be alive."

The man was amused at the idea that the sentiment could be interpreted as disrespectful.

"It's always better to avoid death."

Garnas couldn't quite shake the thought that he *had* died. He held no belief in a paradise waiting for him beyond death; he believed no stories about where his soul would find rest. Maybe being returned to the world, to be with friends again, was the closest he could hope for.

It was enough.

BEN WRIGHT

ACKNOWLEDGEMENTS

I owe Roz and Jo a great deal for taking a look at an early draft of this story, written under difficult circumstances, and convincing me that yes, it was indeed a tale worth telling and that I should continue with it. You opened doors, thank you.

—David Gullen

I'd like to thank my supporters on Patreon, the presence of whom has induced me to write instead of only think about writing. Special mentions go to ShropshireDM on twitch, whose world-building streams were where I trialled some of the ideas in this book, and to Guy Kelly and his delightful band of goblins, for all their encouragement. They're good eggs (enough to put on the pavement, even). Finally, huge thanks to my editor, Jo, and everyone else who beavered away behind the scenes. They're the reason this book exists!

—Ben Wright

ABOUT THE AUTHORS AND EDITORS

David Gullen is a two-times winner of the British Fantasy Society Short Story competition. His work has appeared in magazines, anthologies and podcasts including *F&SF*, *Analog*, & *Parsec*, and reprinted in *The Best of British SF*. His long form work comprises the SF novel, *Shopocalypse*, and the modern fantasy, *The Girl from a Thousand Fathoms*. He lives in South London with his wife, fantasy writer Gaie Sebold, with whom he wrote the charity fundraiser collection *Guru Meditation*. Find out more at www.davidgullen.com.

Ben Wright currently lives in Oxfordshire. Currently he is releasing science-fiction and fantasy stories through Patreon. He has written and performed for local theatre companies and spends a great deal of time playing or writing different kinds of games. He holds a doctorate in statistics, which is about as exciting as you imagine. He's just old enough to remember *The Adventure Game* on BBC2. After ten years' employment in bioinformatics, he's now starting to get some idea of what it actually involves. Shockingly, this includes actual work.

Roz Clarke likes to play around with words; her own and other people's. She has short stories in several anthologies, edits novels for Kristell Ink, and is best known for her editing partnership with Joanne Hall, which has produced such anthologies as *Airship Shape & Bristol Fashion* and the BSFA award-nominated *Fight Like A Girl*. You can twt her at @zora_db, or skeet @rozc.bsky.social.

ROZ CLARKE & JOANNE HALL

Jo Hall was formerly Acquisitions Editor at Grimbold Books and loves working with authors to help them unleash their visions on the world (for good or ill). Her novels have previously been shortlisted for the Tiptree, Lambda and British Fantasy awards. She can be found on Bluesky @ hierath77.bsky.com.

Roz and Jo have been working together since the Bristol F&SF group started running BristolCon, brainchild of the late Colin Harvey, of which Jo was Chair and Roz held various roles on the concom. Both writers and editors in their own right, they first collaborated on *Colinthology*, a memorial anthology for Colin. They now collaborate regularly on wrangling chickens and digging the vegetable beds on their smallholding in South Wales, with their housemate Heather, Jo's partner Chris, and a motley collection of dogs and paperbacks. You can follow their blog on forest gardening and regenerative living at meddwlcoed.wordpress.com.